Peter, the only child of John and Margaret Hunt, was born in Brighton in July 1940 but, at the age of five, began his life as a child in post-war Hong Kong.

At the age of seven, this idyllic life was shattered when he was sent back to England to enrol in a Catholic boarding school in Sussex and later a Catholic boarding public school in Somerset.

His later life was spent in advertising and marketing as well as being the author of five books about Jersey where he now lives with Jennifer, his companion of 20 years.

This memoir is in memory of my parents but also in the memory of the hundreds, perhaps thousands, of colonial parents from the time of the reign of Queen Victoria who made the sacrifice of sending their children back to boarding school in Britain at the age of seven.

It is also in memory of the children, some of whom found life difficult and hated their British education and resented the decisions that their parents had made. Fortunately, I was not one of them because as a child I seemed to have the temperament to just accept whatever was in front of me.

Finally, it is a memory of the two worlds in which I was brought up. On one side was my life at school in England in a post-war era that was grey, rationed and bleak. On the other side was my life in Hong Kong, a vibrant, colourful and booming island life which just seemed full of sunshine.

My personal thanks must go to Annabel von Hofmannsthal and Poppy Eskekilde, both of whom shared my Hong Kong experiences and helped my memory, and to Jennifer, my partner of 20 years, who continued not only to put up with me but also encouraged me to produce this memoir.

Peter Hunt

CHILD OF A BYGONE ERA

AUSTIN MACAULEY PUBLISHERS™

LONDON • CAMBRIDGE • NEW YORK • SHARJAH

A CIP catalogue record for this title is available from the British Library.

ISBN 9781528938495 (Paperback)
ISBN 9781528980456 (ePub e-book)

www.austinmacauley.com

First Published (2021)
Austin Macauley Publishers Ltd
25 Canada Square
Canary Wharf
London
E14 5LQ

Other than personal memories, sources for this book included:

Martin Booth, *Gweilo*, Doubleday (2004)
Vaughan Grylls, *Hong Kong Then and Now*, Pavilion Books (2016)
Auberon Waugh, *Will This Do?*, Century (1991)

Photographic acknowledgements and permissions:

From Peter Hunt's collection:
Downside Abbey, Worth School, Valerie, Hotel Homo, me at 17, my parents, my grandmother, our yacht, my mother and me, Hong Kong Harbour

From *Hong Kong Then and Now*:
Hong Kong Central, Peak Tram, Bank of China, Rickshaws, Star Ferry, Tiger Balm Pagoda

From the internet archives:
Branksome Towers, MV Victoria, Kellett Island, Ladies Recreation Club

Chapter 1

A Memoir of a Colonial Boy

I was born on the 5th of July 1940, in Brighton, a seaside town in the south of England. A few weeks later, the German Luftwaffe unleashed its first and comparatively infrequent bombing display over and into the town. My mother later told me that my father commented: "They are bombing the shit out of this place. We had better move up to London." We moved, me in my swaddling clothes, to a flat in Notting Hill Gate, West London, where we spent the next year of my life, living through the constant German bombardments.

There are only flashes of memory of my early childhood. I do know that when I was two years old, in order to escape the worst of the bombing, we moved to Gerrard's Cross, the home of my godfather and at four years old, we returned to West London, to Wimbledon. From that move to Gerrard's Cross, I remember only falling off my child's bicycle. The scar in my knee is still there to remind me. In Wimbledon, I remember only that I and the other children collected for swapping pieces of shrapnel from destroyed German aircraft. "Swap my piece of a Messerschmitt for a piece of your Junkers," was a popular cry.

The worst and most dramatic memory concerned pain. The bedrooms in our flat were heated by single electric bars set into the wall. One night, I climbed out of my cot, put my right hand on the unlit electric bar and turned it on with my left hand. My screams woke my parents and my mother had to pull my hand off the electric bar. The skin of one of my hands was repaired but, to this day, I have a slightly hooked fourth finger, where the reset was not correctly finished.

Other memories are aided. One night, as happened quite often, the air-raid sirens sounded their alarm and my parents sped down to the neighbourhood's air-raid shelter. My mother asked my father, who, in turn, asked my mother where was their precious only son and heir, Peter. I had been left, gurgling happily, in my pram in a recess under the chimney breast.

My mother was from Durham and came to London in the 1930s as a nurse. She was half Irish, half Scottish and brought up in a mining family. She was an attractive and streetwise lady who met my father on a No 9 bus, was courted and married my father in 1936. As a young bride, she could never have imagined what the next ten years were to bring. Her parenthood has remained a mystery. Many years later, I discovered that she had a number of half-brothers, all miners, some of whom survived the war. That was the most I ever knew of this side of my family.

My driving licence photograph, aged 17

Chapter 2

My father was a chartered accountant in the firm of Peat, Marwick and Mitchell, later to morph into KPMG, one of the largest accounting firms in the world. He was half Italian through his mother and half English through his father.

We are not sure how his mother, who came from a small village called Casino de Castro, an hour's drive north of Rome, arrived in London. The story is that a childless couple of rich Americans somehow arranged to take her on as a daughter and brought her to London. This would have been in the first decade of the 20th century. The Americans suffered a financial disaster, so my grandmother set out to find a rich husband.

Meanwhile, my grandfather, English to the core, whose sole activities seemed to be painting and fishing, came from a middle-class Essex family with a paper business in the City of London. He had three sisters and a brother, all of whom believed that money grew on trees and spent it accordingly. My grandfather needed to find a rich wife.

Oh dear. They met, married, produced my father and realised their financial limitations. My father was given a good education at St Paul's in London, but sometime during this period, my grandmother returned to Italy and my grandfather remained in England. They both met companions who remained with them until their deaths.

My grandmother must have been an attractive, or at least an interesting looking young woman as she became a 'B' actress in early movies. Unfortunately, this had a horrific effect on my father who suffered regular nightmares during his early years.

In those days, children's cinema mornings were held at the local cinema on Saturdays. The programme included news, cartoons and a thriller. To retain the audience, the thriller was divided into two sections, the first, one Saturday, the second the next. My grandmother invariably played the part of the damsel in distress. One week, she would be left tied to the rails as the train came hurtling around a corner towards her. The next, she would be tied to a lift, water rising up the shaft, perilously towards her head. She, of course, was never rescued until the beginning of the second half, a week later, leaving my poor father with his periodic nightmares.

La Nonna, my Italian grandmother

Chapter 3

When war broke out, my father was seconded to the Ministry of Supply and, for his military service, joined the Home Guard. He was made a platoon commander of an anti-aircraft gun on Wimbledon Common, later the home of the Wombles. The only story he ever told me about his war was about his platoon. It was composed of a mismatch of individuals, some with disabilities such as a missing leg or arm, others were locals and others from the East End of London, the Cockneys.

One day, as they marched to their gun emplacement, one of the Cockneys touched my father's arm, swept his hand towards his colleagues and commented: "Fine body of men this lot, Mr H. Should give that bastard 'Itler something to think about." That was all I ever heard from either of my parents about their survival through the five years of the war.

That 'bastard 'Itler' had no intention of reducing his attacks on London and from June to October 1944, London was subjected to a terrifying new weapon – the Doodlebug. The Doodlebug was a jet-propelled, pilotless flying bomb, launched from the coast of France, at the rate of over 100 per day, for the four months of its assault. The noise of their jet engine was the first sign that they were flying in overhead, the moment the sound of the engine stopped, the machine would cease flying and descend to any target underneath. There was no attempt to bomb military targets. This weapon was designed to kill, destroy and demoralise the resistance of the people of London and thereby the British. Their assault ended only when Allied troops reached their bases.

After D day, my father was called up to the head office of Peat's where they had started planning to rebuild their company, now that the war was nearly over. They needed young accountants to staff their overseas offices. My father was approached and offered a job in Hong Kong. The salary and the income-free tax status in Hong Kong was very attractive to a couple with a young child, so my mother insisted that he accepted the post.

At the end of September 1945, after the Japanese capitulation earlier that month, my father departed to set up a home for us and to re-start his professional life as a chartered accountant after the unavoidable five-year interruption.

My parents, John and Margaret

Chapter 4

I was now five and after Christmas, my mother and I boarded the SS Cynthia, a troopship converted into a passenger liner, and began the three-week journey to join up with my father in Hong Kong.

Childhood memories are strange. They come in flashes, sometimes, even when you are asleep. I do, however, remember with perfect clarity the most upsetting disaster that happened to me. I have to admit that I have absolutely no musical talent (at school, I was told to mime the words the others were singing). Why, therefore, I had been given a mouth organ, I had no idea but I took great pleasure in walking around the decks blowing into the mouth organ with great enthusiasm. I think it was on the second day of our journey that my mother tore it from my hands and mouth, and tossed it overboard. I imagine that this was followed by floods of tears.

It was at Aden that I remember boys who looked about my age, would swim by the side of the docked liner and dive for coins, tossed into the water by passengers. I doubt that they still do this today, though, perhaps they still do.

My father had acquired an apartment in Branksome Towers on May Road. May Road is halfway up the Peak and next to the May Road Station of the Peak tram, a funicular railway that climbs up from Victoria, the capital, to the splendid but often fog-bound heights at the top of the Peak – then the area for the homes of the Taipans, or leading European business traders.

May Road sat between two of the major roads from the town to the Peak, the Magazine Gap Road (the point at which one drove over from north to south of the island and dominated by a Naval apartment bloc) and the old Peak Road, a steep direct road, up the north face of the Peak. Buildings were sparse, the only major construction being the Pok Fu Lam reservoir. The hillsides themselves were dominated by wild greenery, home to birds, reptiles and, during the season, hundreds of butterflies.

The view from our apartment, over the city of Hong Kong and across the harbour to Kowloon and the New Territories beyond was spectacular. There was and still maybe is a Trivial Pursuit type question as to where in the world does a Queen look at nine dragons. The Cantonese for nine is *Kow* and dragons are *loon* (Kowloon) and the Queen is Victoria, so the answer is Hong Kong.

The glorious view across Hong Kong's harbour to Kowloon

Chapter 5

I was enrolled in the Peak school, situated a short walk from the uppermost terminal of the Peak tram. This wonderful contraption was drawn by an enormous wheel at the top of the rail track, to which were attached two carriages, one at the top and one at the bottom. As one went up, the other came down, meeting near May Road where the track was separated so each carriage could pass. The wheel track was designed with serrated edges on to which the emergency brake could bite if needed. The carriages were divided into sections, the front one for the Europeans and the back one, open to the elements, for the Chinese. In the covered section, I adored the seats, the backs of which could be switched, so that you sat forward whether going up or down. They made a most satisfactory bang when you thrust them over.

The other peculiarity of the tram was that there were more stations at the lower section than at the upper. The down carriage would suddenly lurch to a stop in the middle of nowhere, much to the surprise of tourists who became uneasy at the strange swinging effect of the carriage on the tracks. There were often looks of relief on the tourists' faces as the tram continued its descent.

Every school day, I would board the tram and enjoy the thrill of being taken up through wild greenery, always at a dramatic angle, to the terminal station at the top. This joyous adventure would be repeated in reverse at the end of the school day, though it was a necessity to stop at the shop in the terminal to purchase bubble gum or sweets or, even, more delicious on a hot day, one of those eating pleasures labelled 'not with parental approval' for the return journey. This was a popsicle, commonly called a popsie, basically an ice lolly, heavy in sugar with milk, or fruit, or even more exotic flavours such as bean paste. They cost 10 cents and were delicious.

Branksome Towers was a large block of flats, built at some height above May Road and approached by a path that was quite a steep climb up to the flats. Enterprising Chinese coolies had set up tiny bamboo shacks by the tram station and they offered lifts to the residents in their sedan chairs or rickshaws for a few cents a journey.

Branksome Towers – halfway up the Peak and home to our
first apartment.

Chapter 6

I had a friend who lived in a house between May Road and our apartment bloc, further over towards the tramway and, therefore, directly over these bamboo shacks. His house had a garden and at the end of the garden, a retaining wall, a flower border and rich, mouldable earth. To my shame, one day the temptation was just too much. We made earth bombs and lobbed them down the hill, onto the bamboo shacks of the coolies. It was the first time that I was called into the bathroom and the hairbrush applied to my posterior by a disappointed and irate father.

Beyond the pathway to our flats and further down the road was one of the centres of our life in Hong Kong – the Ladies Recreation Club, or more commonly, the LRC. This was a veritable haven for young children. There were tennis courts and a pavilion where, for the first time in our young lives, we could sign chits for our snacks and drinks. A swimming pool was being considered and it was eventually completed a year and a half later.

My mother and I soon settled in, though I felt my mother had greater difficulty in getting used to servants than I did. Ah Chook was our number one boy, though he was probably in his late thirties, Ah Li, number two boy and cook, probably in his early thirties, and my best friend in the world Ah Woo, a lady of indeterminate age, who was housemaid and my amah or nanny. All our house servants wore the same uniform, a white tunic type jacket, soft black trousers and soft shoes. Ah Woo, Ah Chook explained to me, was known as a *'saw hei'* amah. *Saw hei* means combed, as they kept their hair in tight buns. They were a sorority of women, originally from mainland China, who had taken a vow of celibacy. I never questioned whether they were successful.

As my mother became wiser in the ways of servants, she learnt that there were particular rules and understandings between staff and management that were scrupulously obeyed to the mutual satisfaction of both parties.

The Ladies Recreation Club in its early days

Chapter 7

Ah Woo had a wooden chest under the bed in her room. During each month, she would acquire from the kitchen a bag of rice or some soap or sugar or toilet paper, even a roast chicken, items that she considered were rewards for services beyond her wages and they would be stored in her wooden box. At the end of each month, my mother would send her out to the market or to take me somewhere and enter Ah Woo's room and open her wooden chest. She would then remove half the items and return them into stock. On Ah Woo's return, she and my mother would smile at each other, Ah Woo might even make a small bow knowing that honour had been satisfied on both sides.

Chinese cooks seem to have an innate excellence in creating canapés, called in Hong Kong 'small chow'. When my parents would give a cocktail or dinner party, every table in the reception room would have its tin of cigarettes and its Ronson table lighter. Table and ceiling fans would be on their highest settings and ice machines would be in full blast. Ah Li and Ah Woo would have spent hours preparing delicious and excitingly designed canapés. Ah Chook as head boy, only oversaw these activities but, by constant sampling, ensured that the canapés met his high standards.

One other of Ah Chook's duties and my favourite was that only he was allowed to take around the canapés to the guests once they had been handed to him by Ah Li. He would tour the room and continue down to my bedroom where I would be reading some momentarily favoured comic to ensure that I too sampled the delights from the kitchen. On these occasions, I was a very happy and spoilt child but never a very slim one.

The Chinese relationship at that time between themselves and their employers was based on the Cantonese sense of honour. I believe there was affection, certainly, there was for children and, if not affection, then at least respect for most Europeans.

This sense of honour had a peculiar logic. During the 1940s, there were rumours that the Chinese were planning a rebellion against the Europeans, who, when the rebellion started, were to kill the Europeans in their beds.

Chapter 8

My father called in Ah Chook to ask whether if the rebellion took place, he really would kill my father, my mother and little Peter. Ah Chook looked horrified and told my father that he would never do such an outrageous thing. However, he went on to explain that he had come to an arrangement with the number one boy in the adjoining apartment that if such an event occurred, he would kill the inhabitants of that apartment and their boy would carry out this ghastly task in his place.

Fortunately, this rebellion never took place.

The LRC was one centre of activity for mothers and children alike. The other for me was the Hong Kong yacht club, a boatyard and clubhouse built on a tiny island called Kellett Island, just off the waterfront near Causeway Bay and the Royal Navy's dockyards. My father was a keen sailor and progressed from dinghies, though dragons to Princesses, a type of yacht that he claimed to have been involved in its design. I have never had any reason to disbelieve him. It was the dragon that I was allowed to sail even as a child, as long as I was accompanied by our boat boy, Ah Ling.

To reach the yacht club, a small fleet of sampans nestled close to the sewage outlet that ran near the steps, down to the water, who, for an agreed fee, rowed members the short trip across to the island and when signalled back, again to shore. By the time I was a teenager, the sewage outlet had been closed and a road built across to the club, the wall becoming part of the extended marina and typhoon shelter. Such progress, sadly, saw the demise of the sampans and their noisy, gossipy, life-hardened lady rowers. My amah, Ah Woo, really only spoke to me in Cantonese and, as I had a child's ear for different languages, I picked up a smattering of Cantonese. One of the joys of being ferried by the sampan women was bantering with them as they lived, as far as I could tell, on their sampans and made their living either by ferrying us to and fro, or from the nearby sewage outlet.

Kellett Island – home to the Hong Kong Yacht Club

Chapter 9

Human manure, known as night soil, was a standard fertiliser for the local Hong Kong and Kowloon crop fields. Products from these fields, for obvious reason, were shunned by Europeans, who shopped in only specific stores or markets that claimed not to use 'night soil' as a fertiliser.

The harbour was constantly in motion, alive like an ants' nest. The Star and Yaumati ferries crossed or set off for outlying quays. Junks of seasoned teak, three-masted and up to 80 feet long and 20 feet wide, sailed majestically on their way to trade, often home to three generations of family and their livestock. Inshore, sampans scuttled everywhere whilst water taxis known as walla-wallas bustled amongst the traffic. Through all this, would weave yachts and pleasure boats and tugs, manoeuvring large cargo lighters to their go-downs or waterside warehouses. Then the big boys would arrive, the ocean-going freighters, the passenger liners and the lions of the harbour – the war vessels of the British Navy and the American Pacific fleet.

Sailing one day, past the bulk of an American aircraft carrier, I was hailed from somewhere far above to come aboard. I waved cheerfully as I sailed past. A few days later, when I returned to the yacht club, there was an invitation from the captain for the kid in the dragon and three of his friends to come and visit the aircraft carrier. Parental permission was required but for the four of us, we could not have been more excited as we considered this an enormous privilege, setting us apart from our mundane friends.

We were met in a very smart motor launch, carrying the star and stripes flag and a beautifully uniformed young man who was our guide around this incredible piece of fighting machinery. On the bridge, we were introduced to the captain who explained that he and his sons sailed dragons in their home in America, so he felt only duty-bound to extend the hand of friendship to other dragon sailors. Though the sentiment was a bit beyond me, I thanked him kindly and we were taken off to the high spot of the whole trip – our introduction to hot dogs and hamburgers, both covered in lashings of tomato ketchup. Our usual soft drink was Green Spot or Watson's orangeade. Here, we were also introduced to Coca Cola, which I quite liked but was never hooked on. This example of American hospitality has influenced my feelings for Americans as the most generous of people and has stayed with me for the rest of my life.

Chapter 10

Christmas was upon us and my father was on the yacht club's entertainment committee. To welcome the New Year, there was to be a ball and as the high spot, I was to be brought into the ballroom as New Year itself, in a specially designed seven-foot dinghy. The dinghy was so designed that, after the event, it could be made seaworthy. It was then announced, after my dramatic entrance, that the dinghy was to be named Peter and given to me as a thank you gift. I am sure this maybe have been an impromptu decision, occasioned by the excess of alcohol consumed that evening, but you have to know that there was no happier six-year-old in the world that night.

As a child, other than my amah and our house and boat boys, I had very little interaction or knowledge of the Chinese who surrounded us. I just accepted what I now realise was apartheid. Chinese businessmen were not allowed into any of the European clubs and Chinese women and children were not allowed into any of our recreational clubs. On the Star ferry, the most popular way to travel between Hong Kong and Kowloon and on the trams, Chinese travelled on the lower floor, Europeans on the top. I understood, not quite knowing where this information came from, that prior to the end of the War, only Europeans had houses at the top of the Peak and on the summit of Hong Kong's other inhabited island, Cheung Chow.

At the LRC if we played tennis, we had Chinese boys who picked up the balls and handed them back to us. At the yacht club, we had a ten-pin bowling alley. Here a Chinese boy would set up the pins, return the bowls and reset the pins each time we bowled. In truth, we children lived in surroundings that were natural to us because we had experienced no other. My English contemporaries were suffering the hardships of rationing and the immediate post-war years. We were benefitting from American generosity, a booming economy and an acquiescent local population who appeared to be there to ensure our life in the colonies was as smooth and as delightful as possible.

And as children, we may have suffered from heat rash, but even that was temporary and soon forgotten. Factor 15, parental love and amahs are wonderful things!

Me at New Year's Eve with my mother

Chapter 11

My parents, on the other hand, did become very good friends with various Chinese families through business contacts originally, but my knowledge of them was very limited as I was not expected to fraternise with any Chinese children and there were none at my school.

One of my parents' friends was a very rich businessman called Lee Choc Li. One day, we were invited to his palatial mansion, overlooking Repulse Bay on the south side of the island. To entertain his children, he had bought them mini motor cars with real petrol engines that his children could drive around the garden. Lee Choc Li invited me to drive one and whilst showing me the controls, by mistake, he burned my hand with his cigarette. I burst into tears. He was full of apologies so to appease me and hopefully to dry my tears, he gave me the little motor car. Tears changed, surprisingly quickly, to those of joy and gratitude. Unfortunately, my father intervened and forbade the gift, my only consolation now being an enormous ice cream. It took me a while to forgive a man whom I considered at that moment to be a harsh and uncaring father.

As well as sailing and playing tennis, we young children were given the opportunity to learn to play golf. The club kind enough to encourage our pretty futile efforts was a 9-hole course at Deep Water Bay, now part of the Hong Kong Golf Club. Each of us children was accompanied by our amah who, whilst keeping a weather eye on us, immensely enjoyed these outings. They immediately congregated into a gaggle and kept up an inexhaustible supply of chatter and gossip, interspersed with cackles of laughter and probably rude comments on the men working on the golf course and its surrounds. The result of this was that Ah Woo was almost servile to my mother if a day for golf was promoted. It seemed to be even more pleasing to her than their mutual understanding of the monthly movement of household goods.

My favourite method of transport – the Peak Tram

Chapter 12

Our family day was Sunday. There were really only two choices. The first was to have a Sunday lunch at home followed at my father's insistence for a 'constitutional' two-mile walk around the top of the Peak. The second, which was much more to my liking, was to set off on the yacht and to anchor in a bay to swim or to explore ashore. Depending on wind and tide, we would choose Clear Water Bay (aptly named as one could see the sand some ten to fifteen feet below) for swimming or sail to the other side of Hong Kong, to the islands of Lamma, Cheung Chow or Lantau. My least favourite was Lamma as it was virtually unpopulated by humans, but seriously populated by snakes. Cheung Chow was a mini-Hong Kong, the only other island settled by Europeans and Lantau, the largest island in the Hong Kong area was also scarcely populated, mainly by fishermen.

Lunch on the yacht invariably included my favourite, a prawn curry. Kept hot in cylindrical steel containers; it was served with a selection of titbits brought on board in bamboo or rattan mini suitcases, a feature of picnic life in Hong Kong.

I suppose, as children, we just accepted our style of life which was pleasant in the extreme. As I went to bed each night, I would undress and drop my clothes on a chair or the floor and Ah Woo would follow me collecting them. New ones were laid out in the morning. Pyjamas would be warm and laid out next to Teddy on the pillow. Within the limits set by my parents, any request of mine for food or drink, or for anything really, was supplied.

Only one thing would cause unpleasantness and that was the weather. Hong Kong in the summer could be both, very hot and very humid. Our flat was cooled by electric fans both on the ceiling and on the tables (air conditioning was new and only present in some offices). Though our rooms were spacious with a large veranda overlooking the harbour, my father had decorated it as if we lived in Kent or Sussex. The walls were wood-panelled, furniture was of solid wood and our sofas and chairs were in traditional English prints. This was fine at the front of the apartment but my bedroom was at the back. The only rooms further back were the servants' quarters. The heat would build as it progressed through the apartment. The only relief was the whirr of the ceiling fan and the loss of the blankets that had been needed in the cool winter months.

Chapter 13

The other, rather more dramatic weather concern was a Tai Fung, or in English a typhoon. The typhoon season was from May to October and if and when it hit directly, it caused serious damage to property and to community services.

Descending one day home from school, I became aware that something out of the ordinary was happening. The coolies and their huts at our station had gone and there was a feeling of impending disaster in the air. Everything seemed too still, too quiet. Arriving home, all the furniture had been moved indoors from the veranda and Ah Chook and Ah Li were sealing our windows with shutters. On asking what was happening, my mother explained that a big storm, a typhoon, was forecast for that night.

It was just about as I was falling asleep that the wind picked up speed and howled around our block of flats. Then came the rain, lashing against the building as if there was nothing in the world but wind and rain and a sheltering world.

I fell asleep to find that the weather had cleared in the morning. On enquiry, my mother explained that we had been lucky. The centre of the typhoon had passed to the east one hundred miles away, so we had suffered only the outer edge of the storm. I didn't admit to my mother that I regretted falling asleep as I had found the roar of the wind and the rain to be very exciting. I have loved storms, admittedly not typhoons, ever since.

As a child, these discomforts were taken in the same spirit as the multiple pleasures that accompanied most days. Even school was a pleasure to attend and we knew, both boys and girls, that somehow we were privileged.

In early 1947, the next momentous decision in my life was taken by my parents. I was to be sent back to boarding school in England. As a child, I really had no knowledge of any religious persuasion my parents might have held. I am quite sure we never went to church, so it was not until I was told that in the Autumn I was to go to England, to a Roman Catholic school called Worth Priory in Sussex, that I thought I might be a Catholic.

Chapter 14

With a child's fortitude, I looked on this as an adventure, never realising that my childhood would never be the same again.

Passengers by sea had a choice whether to travel on a luxury liner or to travel on a freighter. In those days, freighters were, and possibly still are, international workhorses, plying their trade along coasts and across oceans. They were basically cargo vessels but would have accommodation for 10 to 12 passengers. My parents chose a freighter to return my mother and me back to England. It was an incredible journey.

We left Hong Kong travelling to Yokohama in Japan, then across the Pacific to San Francisco, south via Los Angeles to Colon, through the Panama Canal, passing Panama City and ending this first leg of our journey in New York. After a few days there, we took the Queen Mary for the last leg of this momentous journey.

Life at sea was pretty simple for us passengers. There were no frills and no exotic entertainments but there was good food, excellent accommodation and simple pleasures such as Canasta and good books and for me, the run of the whole vessel, from the engine room to the bridge. An added bonus was the new world of the ports that we reached and at which we offloaded a cargo or imported a new one.

I still wish that I had been slightly older as my memory is necessarily restricted but certain highlights remain with me to this day.

At our first stop, Yokohama, my mother and I left the boat and took a train to Tokyo to stay with some friends of my parents. Their house fascinated me as it appeared to be made of wood and paper. Each room seemed to be separated by sliding wooden doors with walls made of very thin, almost translucent paper, allowing as much light as possible into each room. The bathroom and lavatory were affixed to the outside of the house and also seemed to be made of paper, though less translucent. I had never experienced a house like it and, I feel sure, never will again.

Chapter 15

Later, I asked my mother about this type of house. She understood that they were made from simple lightweight materials because this area of Japan was subject to earthquakes. If one struck the house, it might collapse, but no serious damage was done. One day, I must find out if this is true.

During the long crossing from Yokohama to the West coast of America, I was befriended by the crewmembers, in particular the cook, who invariably found excellent titbits for elevenses and for, as he called it, 'fourzees' and also by the leading deckhand. I also had a sneaking suspicion that my mother might have been befriended by one of the officers but my friends were the crew. I ranged all over the freighter, even given a simple task to carry out such as checking the security of the cargoes in the holds or steering the vessel through uneventful seas. In fact, we were very lucky in that; we enjoyed reasonable weather throughout this journey across and southwards down the Pacific.

Our first stop was in San Francisco. My crew friends insisted that I join them for a trip which included dropping off all the dirty laundry, then continuing past Alcatraz Island, over the Golden Gate bridge (not golden by the way), up to

San Quentin, down through Albany and back through downtown San Francisco. The journey took all day and was wondrous. I did wonder on viewing two prison sites in one day if it held any relevance to the past lives of my crew friends but I wisely left the question unasked.

In Los Angeles, laundry again had to be dropped off and was an excellent excuse to join my friends in touring the city. The port of Los Angeles is well, to the south of the city and I must admit that I did not find it nearly as interesting as San Francisco. It just seemed to be a maze of streets and avenues. However, always having an interest in food and drink, I was introduced to a chocolate malt. This is a luxurious, creamy concoction made from vanilla ice cream, chocolate syrup, milk and malt powder. It is very rich and no doubt laden with calories. (In later life, it would be the first thing that I would order on arriving in America – just as a ham and cheese baguette played the same role in France.)

We chugged on to Colon and the Panama Canal and the wonder of this short cut, built in 1919, between the two mighty oceans.

Chapter 16

To a boy who has never seen or, indeed, had any idea of locks to have, two within days of each other was heavenly. The first lock lifted our freighter up to Lake Gaston, an ascent of 85 ft or 26 metres, the second lowered it down again to the Atlantic Ocean and, passing Panama City, we headed north to New York.

New York proved to be a disaster, not for what it is, but for one event that happened and I have never worked out why my mother chose it. Having visited the Statue of Liberty, the Empire State Building and the Rockefeller Centre, my mother decided as a special treat that we would go to a show at the Radio City Music Hall.

First, there was a live musical show featuring the Rockettes, a troupe of extremely attractive, young female dancers which I thoroughly enjoyed. This was followed by a film entitled 'The Snake Pit' featuring Olivia de Havilland. The story was the mental deterioration of the heroine who was imprisoned in a lunatic asylum. I expect that there was villainy afoot, but she was diagnosed as totally insane and condemned to the lowest level of the asylum, the snake pit. Here she was put in a straitjacket and left in a padded cell. It was at this point that I began to scream and cry. I was hastily removed and had nightmares for the next month or so. What on earth my mother had in mind when she took me to this horror, I have no idea. Maybe she liked Olivia de Havilland. Who knows! There was an upside which is that I really did enjoy the Rockettes and have liked this type of show dancing ever since.

The comparison between our freighter home for two months and the Queen Mary could not have been more marked. She was Cunard's flagship and designed for luxury sea travel. New to us was air conditioning throughout the passenger sections, a swimming pool, a variety of restaurants accompanied by entertainments and impeccable service. There was even a small hospital and a squash court. This was a far cry from the simple pleasures of our freighter but, to be honest, I missed terribly the freedoms I had enjoyed on our Pacific adventure and the excitement of visiting new ports.

Chapter 17

We arrived in early September in Southampton, to a grey, drizzling day and started on the steam train from Southampton to London where we were to stay with my grandfather. This was not the bright, dramatic weather of Hong Kong. This was miserable and during the couple of weeks we were in London, we were introduced to 'smog'. Smog was a disgusting mixture of coal, smoke and fog. It was so thick that you could not see your hand in front of your face and you had to cover your mouth and nose with, at the very least, a handkerchief so as not to breathe in the filth. Not only was it disgusting, it was frightening as you could so easily lose your way in parts of the city not well known to you. Fortunately, the times that I was caught in it, I had my mother by my side.

The day came, the 14th of September, when my mother took me to Victoria Station. I had on my cap, jacket, shirt and tie with shorts and smart new K leather shoes and carried my suitcase with my worldly goods, not much, within. On the platform, I was introduced to a man in long black robes whose hand I had to shake, who introduced himself as Father Jerome and said that he was to be my housemaster. Not sure what to make of this, I turned to my mother only to notice that she kept applying her handkerchief to her eyes, determined not to cry in front of me. She gave me one last hug, handed me to the monk and turned quickly away. I can only imagine her anguish. Her husband was half a world away and her only child was being sent off to a boarding school. Her only child, however, as instructed, climbed into a carriage full of other 'new' boys more curious to find out what he had been let in for, than worrying about his mother. He had no idea that he would not see her again until the end of term, nearly three months away.

Though, enjoying a reasonable life in Hong Kong, my parents were not wealthy. They had no family money behind them. It was necessary, therefore, for my mother to find some kind of employment that would give me a home during the holidays whilst my father stayed in Hong Kong until his annual vacation. The holiday arrangement for professionals in the Far East in those days was to take very short local holidays but for longer holidays you could take a four-month leave every four years or a six-month leave every six years.

The impressive drive up to the entrance of Worth School

Chapter 18

My mother found the position of lady's companion to a widow, Mrs Stanton, in the village of Corfe Castle in Dorset. I have no idea whether my mother was paid a salary, but she had a home, looked after rather than nursed Mrs Stanton, and was the housekeeper and cook. It was to be my holiday home for the following year.

As the train steamed out of Victoria, heading south to Sussex, it was the start of eight years of education with the Benedictine monks, four at the preparatory school Worth in Sussex and later four at Downside, the Public School in Somerset.

I had not been prepared to discover that Worth was a very beautiful school. It had once been one of Lord Cowdray's country estates, the main buildings being set in 500 acres of lush Sussex countryside, complete with a ha-ha, ponds and fields. Downside purchased it in 1932, to create a priory and preparatory school as a feeder to its public school.

We entered in our coach through the front gates, the ha-ha wall on our right until we turned left through another set of gates and approached the quadrangle in front of the original main house. (A ha-ha wall is a type of sunken wall giving the illusion of a continuous lawn whilst providing a boundary to the fields beyond.)

We were greeted by the headmaster Dom Maurice Bell and taken into the large assembly hall to the right of the front door. Here, we were introduced to Matron, and allocated our dormitory, a building separate from the main buildings and reached by a short walk up a hill. We slept over the stables for the school's horses. As new boys, we were here a day ahead of the elder pupils – able to at least find our way about before looking too stupid in front of our peers.

The very first harsh lesson and this on the first night was that the school did not employ amahs. As I went to my dormitory bed, I shred my clothes as I had done at home. No one picked them up. A loud voice called 'Hunt' from the far end of the dormitory, a master appeared and told me, in no uncertain terms, to pick up my clothes, fold them and put them in my bedside locker. Lesson learnt.

Chapter 19

The second lesson, actually a series of lessons, was my introduction to Roman Catholicism. We attended Low Mass three times a week, but on Sundays, we attended both Low and High mass. The Mass was said in Latin, the opening words of which – I still remember to this day – were *Introibo ad altare Dei*. We were given our missal and catechism, only the Missal lasting me through both schools and we were to receive one RI or Religious Instruction lesson per week. I heard somewhere that St Ignatius Loyola, the founder of the Jesuits had stated: "Give me the child for the first seven years and I will give you the man." I rather thought that I was glad to be with the Benedictines.

The school was divided into the old and the new parts, separated by a hill that climbed up to the approach road, over which were the playing fields and before which was our dormitory, the stables, the gym and a cinema. The original building housed the church, dining room, library, assembly hall, headmaster's study, other studies and the masters' common room. A further part of the original buildings was the Priory, home to the monks. Our teachers were a mixture of monks and lay teachers, the only woman amongst them being Matron who became a great favourite in all our lives for her interest and gentleness with all our problems and ailments.

I am sure I did not do it intentionally, but I seemed to make friends with those who could prove useful to me. Having written this, my very best friend was called Ambrose Rigby, who was of no use to me whatsoever except to be my very best friend. However, friend Anthony Witham's parents had been interned by the Japanese in the Stanley camp in Hong Kong and returned to England after the war. They lived in the nearby town of Haywards Heath and would take pity on me by inviting me to their home for holidays after my mother had returned to Hong Kong. Another great friend was Michael Church. He had a large family that lived in Weybridge. They were kind enough to do the same thing.

Chapter 20

The academic year was split into three terms: winter, Easter and summer. They were each approximately 13 weeks long. Other than one short weekend per term and the annual sports day, parents were not involved overtly in our curricular activities. The one short weekend was strange for us colonials. If no friendly parent was prepared to take us back home with their beloved, we stayed at the school. We called ourselves 'the lost cause', one of my better phrases, and enjoyed ourselves enormously, having the whole school to ourselves.

Sports were compulsory, rugby in the winter term, hockey in the Easter term and cricket or tennis in the summer term. Gym was also compulsory, the gym being arranged with various implements of torture such as ropes, wall bars, wooden horses and other gymnastic implements. Gym was not my favourite activity and one I was never good at.

Once a week, we went to the cinema. In the winter, once we had progressed to dormitories in the main school, we would walk up the hill, to the cinema in scarves and overcoats as the inside of the cinema was as cold as the outside. We carried torches to see our way as there was no lighting between the schoolhouse and the cinema buildings.

I remember only one lesson. This was English, my favourite subject and one that the master whose name may have been Peter Whigham, taught us and which left me with a lasting love for the English language and culture. His was always our last lesson on Saturday mornings and rather than delving into a specific topic, he would read short stories to us. My favourite then and now were the stories of a writer called Saki. They are now dated, but continue to be very amusing and are representative of the era just before that of my parents.

Saturday evenings were the evenings when those of us who had parents abroad, had to sit down and write to them. I still have somewhere an old blue, airmail letter. It allowed you about 300 words and it was often quite difficult to fill it up with weekly news. My writing became larger, the more term went on.

England in those days was heavily rationed. Virtually, everything including food and clothing was rationed. We, as boys, were never conscious of this limitation whilst we were at school. We were well fed and clothed, though there was no such thing as central heating, so living with being cold was a daily event and bed was the very best place to be in the cold winter nights.

Chapter 21

We seemed to slip easily into the ways and customs of a boys' school. This one, fortunately, a very happy one. There was a set curriculum for lessons, all preparing us for the common entrance exam, the results of which would decide whether we were educated enough to enter a public school. We were streamed into classroom grades, Grade A, being for the cleverest and Grade D, for the least clever. I never made grade A, but then I didn't make Grade D either.

Once established as a pupil and knowing where to go and when life became much more regulated – school, sports, sleep. We were subject to the normal illnesses of children including mumps and measles and chickenpox, all of which meant a confinement under the tender care of Matron. It is fair to say that I looked forward to ailments as long as they were not too serious as isolation and tender care suited me and reminded me of life with my amah.

Initially, the weeks passed slowly and then, just as with a holiday, the time speeded up, the weeks passed and the end of my first term arrived.

I had survived.

The term was over and I was on my way to Christmas in Corfe Castle with my mother and the as yet unknown, Mrs

Stanton. Much to my embarrassment, my mother who was waiting for me at Victoria Station, hugged and kissed me in front of a group of returning schoolboys. Fortunately, other mothers behaved in much the same way, so I allowed myself to feel delighted at this show of maternal affection. Together, we taxied to Waterloo to take the train to Wareham where we changed onto the branch line to Corfe Castle. Having disembarked there, the train steamed off to its terminus at the seaside town of Swanage.

There was something magical about travelling in a steam train. The smoke constantly plumed and streamed past the window of the swaying carriage as it clacked its way over the joints in the rails. I, delighted in lowering the window and, despite parental warnings, sticking my head out to watch the countryside and on bends the engine itself reliably pulling us over the miles of track. Stations flashed by so quickly that you could not decipher their names. At other times, the country seemed to stand still as field followed field until interrupted abruptly by a bridge or tunnel.

To keep me further entertained, having read about the author Somerset Maugham and his book-bag, I also kept a satchel in which were the latest copies of the Beano and Dandy, a Leslie Charters Saint book, a Dennis Wheatley Thriller and, perhaps, an Arthur Ransome.

Chapter 22

We arrived at Corfe Castle and after a short walk from the station, I was introduced to Mrs Stanton and my new home. Mrs Stanton was a slim, grey-haired lady who seemed very pleasant, my opinion of her improving greatly when, from time to time, she would slip a shilling (5p) into my palm with a finger to her lips to indicate silence, the conspiracy being strictly between ourselves. Her house was pleasantly appointed on a hill that climbed out of the centre of Corfe Castle towards Swanage with a reasonably large garden in which to play at the rear.

The village of Corfe Castle was dominated by a hill on which stood the dramatic remains of a Norman castle, built in the eleventh century by William, the Conqueror. From the remains of its old walls, you looked northwards over the plains of the isle of Purbeck where villages with charming names, like Piddletrenthide, nestled. Descending, you arrived in the main square, the heart of the village, with its newsagent and general store. One road continued down the side of the hill, running northward towards Wareham, the only other two ran southwards towards the high ground, between Corfe Castle and Swanage.

Here, the newsagent became the centre of my life. Stan Hawkins was the proprietor, a veteran of the war who took a kind interest in me, so that I was allowed to help in his shop. Even more exciting, he was an avid fan of Speedway and we would occasionally go in his van to Poole, our closest town, to the stadium where the Poole Pirates race.

Speedway is for motorcycles, their main feature being that the bikes have only one gear and no brakes. Their drivers tear around a dirt track, using their booted feet and their balance as the means of turning at high speed around the corners and along the straights. It is a noisy, fuel-filled, smelly, exciting madness. I never had any idea who had won or lost, but who cared. I was enthralled to be a part of it and enjoyed enormously our occasional race nights.

Stan Hawkins, like my father, only mentioned the war to me once. It seems he was a non-commissioned officer and he and his colleagues were fighting their way up the Italian peninsula when they came across a farmhouse, left deserted by the retreating Germans. In it, they found a cellar full of unlabelled bottles containing red liquid. Was this wine or vinegar? Their only option was to open and test each one. If wine, they thought it was only proper to drink it. If vinegar, they would stick the corks back in and kindly leave the bottle for the next troops who might enter the cellar. He did profess, however, that there were not many bottles left with their corks put back into them.

Chapter 23

My mother's main relaxations were reading, knitting and listening to the wireless. She became a great fan of the Archers and she was not to be disturbed during their early transmissions.

Her other interest was in Scottish dancing. In the village, there was a weekly evening meeting at the village hall. I was dragged along, originally with little interest and clutching a comic. However, the music and the movement began to appeal and I have to admit that I became quite a dab hand (or is it foot) at dancing the jigs, reels and Strathspey reels.

Christmas came and went and, in far too short a time, it was the moment for me to return to school. The journey was reversed and happily meeting my school friends from the previous term at Victoria Station, we boarded the train and made as much noise as possible on our return to school.

At the end of my first year at school, my mother returned to Hong Kong and I was farmed out to an elderly couple called the Podmores, who lived in a small village called Combwich, pronounced Cummage, near Bridgewater in Somerset. Their house was a few miles outside the village and approached down a narrow lane at the end of which was a cattle farm in which I was to spend most of my holiday time.

Mrs Podmore had Portuguese parentage and was a well-built lady who sailed rather than walked. Her husband, on the other hand, was a small lithe man who perennially smoked his pipe and listened to the radio. They were very kind, but somewhat old fashioned. You did not go to the lavatory. You went to read Shakespeare, a complete edition of which sat on the window shelf of the lavatory.

There was no mains electricity, the house electricity being created by a generator which was turned off when they went to bed. Subsequently, for many years, I read under the bedclothes with a torch. Not strange, therefore that some years later, I began to wear glasses.

Chapter 24

About this time, Radio Luxembourg, began broadcasting on 208 metres medium wave. It was the first station to transmit pop songs on a regular basis and its showpiece programme was the English Top Twenty. This programme was broadcast on Sunday night at 11 pm. to midnight or when the clocks changed from midnight to one am. It was the closest thing to Heaven for us young kids and to admit that you had no knowledge of that week's top twenty was to commit yourself to temporary exile.

My only problem was that once I had been put to bed, I was expected to go to sleep. How, then, to set the alarm so that I would wake up at 11 pm. or midnight, depending on the season? The answer was that everything came into bed with me, my radio, my alarm clock, my headphones, my book and my torch. I never knew whether the Podmores knew that I had such an interest in the Top Twenty, but if they did, they were kind enough never to mention it.

The Eagle comic, the first edition of which I had read when in Corfe Castle, remained one of my favourites but rather more adult publications began to appeal. One was Health and Efficiency, a curiously innocent nudist magazine but which introduced us young males to pictures of female breasts and photoplay, full of sensual photographs of all our favourite female stars. Photoplay could be left around the house but H and E, as it was affectionately known, had to be well hidden from prying eyes.

My days were filled with one or two activities, other than the odd shopping expedition to Bridgewater with Mrs Podmore. Obviously, I was growing so the shopping concentrated on clothing and shoes. When you went to buy shoes, the retailers had x-ray machines for your feet. You would put your feet into the machine and peer down at the outline of your shoes and your bony toes within. You would think that with this science, considered extremely modern then, that your shoes would fit. They may have done but my toes have never been perfectly straight ever since.

Chapter 25

The first of my habitual activities was bicycling. On a bicycling day after breakfast, Mr Podmore would slip me a sixpence and Mrs Podmore would say, "Enjoy yourself. We'll see you back for tea." I would don my backpack in which would be a flask of water, a book or magazine and a sandwich and off I would cycle. Combwich sat by the River Parrett that flowed through Bridgewater to its mouth at the Bristol Channel. The surrounding countryside was reasonably flat and I normally headed north up to the mouth of the river where I could watch the boating traffic sailing by. Other times, I would find a place to sit and take out my sandwich and book. Bucolic days indeed. They were also innocent days and all the parents that I stayed with had no fear (unlike these days) for their children cycling unchaperoned around the countryside.

My other major activity was helping on the Trotts' cattle farm. The Trotts had two sons in their early twenties who came, I think, to consider me as their pet. They would let me help with the milking, now being done by machine, but every now and again, they would show me how to milk by hand. Mrs Trott was a large family woman, who believed that working men should eat well. It was quite often that I would have a boiled egg for breakfast at the Podmores, then join in a breakfast of ham, eggs, mushroom, tomatoes, toast and tea in their warm and welcoming stone-flagged kitchen which I would have to work off during the rest of the morning in manual labour around the farm.

I continue to be grateful to those who looked after me on my holidays while at Worth School and when I was neither with my parents on their English leave nor back at home in Hong Kong.

Summer arrived and I was to return to Hong Kong. This was to be a great adventure as I had never travelled before without my mother so I was labelled 'an unaccompanied minor'. My grandfather collected me from Victoria Station and taxied me to the BOAC terminal at Heathrow. This was one of a series of tented marquees to the north of the west/east runway. My grandfather kindly gave me a one-pound note. "To help smooth the journey," he said. Grateful as I was, I was not sure how or where I was going to spend it. My hand was shaken and I was passed over to a young lady in a BOAC uniform who relieved me of my suitcase and introduced me to an imposing man with splendid moustaches who she explained was the Captain in-charge of flying us on the first leg of our journey.

Chapter 26

The Captain handed me to another uniformed young man, who explained that he was the co-pilot, one of a flying crew of four, the two pilots, a navigator and a radio operator. We were to fly in a DC4, known as an Argonaut, a four petrol-engine aircraft which unlike its predecessor, the DC3, now had a nose wheel which meant we did not have to climb up the aircraft from the entrance at the rear, but mounted steps directly up to the fuselage. Our route would take us to Rome, Beirut, Delhi, Calcutta, Rangoon, Bangkok and Hong Kong. The flight would take three days and we would land at least twice to overnight in a hotel as the aircraft did not have approved navigation aids for night flying.

There seemed to be a general understanding that we were ready to go and accompanied by my stewardess and the other passengers, we boarded the aircraft to take our seats. I noticed that smoking was forbidden until we were airborne so those who had desperately dragged on their last puff, threw their butts into a large metal container outside the marquee. I had no such aid to alleviate my nerves so was at least grateful for the sweet that was offered before take-off.

Once settled, the four Rolls Royce engines were fired up and we taxied out to the end of the runway. The power increased and we gathered speed down the runway, admittedly with my hands gripping the front of the seat, until the aircraft rose up into the air. I was on my first long haul three-day flight home.

The seats were roomy and comfortable, the stewardesses young and attractive (memories of the Rockettes) and the food reasonable, but the noise from the engines was noticeable and once we reached cruising height, it seemed that virtually every passenger lit a cigarette, even some cigarillos. I could only settle in with my Eagle and other comics, a Leslie Charteris Saint thriller and occasional drinks of orange squash, lemon or lime squash and Coca Cola.

The journey began to be interminable and I began to look forward to landing and taking-off at the various airports at which we stopped and at which we were parked in the transit lounge until re-boarding – the only real change of scenery whilst we were on flying time.

Our first overnight stop was at Beirut where we were bussed to our hotel, fed and, in my case, put to bed. Ensuring that I was tucked in safely, one of the attractive stewardesses was given the chore (short straw) of reading me a bedtime story, ensuring that my pillow was puffed up nicely and that I was ready to go to sleep. To my delight, this enjoyable experience was repeated at our next overnight stop at the Great Eastern Hotel in Calcutta.

Chapter 27

At last, we approached through the gap between the hills of Sam Ka Tsuen and Sai Wan Shan, losing height as we approached over the harbour, towards the Kowloon hills. Turning sharply to avoid the hills, the aircraft descended to Kai Tak's runway and taxied to the terminal building. My first long-distance flight was successfully concluded and I had only been airsick (I am sure from boredom) once.

My parents were waiting for me and, once I had cleared immigration and collected my suitcase, we walked from the terminal, across the runway to a wharf where our yacht and a grinning Ah Ling were there to sail us across the harbour. What an exotic way to be welcomed home!

The next surprise was that we did not take the path up to Branksome Towers, but carried along May Road towards the LRC and to our new home, a block of flats called Aviemore Court. It was a small block, no more than eight apartments but much more spacious and, wonder of wonders, there was window air conditioning in each of the three bedrooms.

As to décor, nothing else had changed. The apartment still had the look of an English country house. To my father, home was England. To me, home was Hong Kong. I think my mother thought quite differently. To her, home was where her husband was, particularly after the years of separation when she had to be away from him looking after me.

The last delight of this homecoming was the welcome from our three servants, who looked just the same and were smiling, bowing and in Ah Woo's case hugging and crying at the return of the 'young master'. Quite enough for one day to turn my head.

Once I had settled in, which included a quick trip to the Peak on the Peak tram, I decided that I was old enough to discover more of my surroundings, particularly in the Central area and along the harbour frontage. At the LRC, the swimming pool had now been completed and a character called Billy Tingle, an ex-champion boxer and well-known bon viveur, had been employed to teach the young children to swim. He also taught sports on a Saturday morning at the cricket club situated in Statue Square, the centre of business Hong Kong and proudly presided over by a statue of Queen Victoria and the Cenotaph. I enrolled for the duration of the holiday.

The heart of Central – the Cenotaph and the Hong Kong Club

Chapter 28

Two of my favourite modes of travel were the Peak tram (obviously) and the Star Ferry. I considered my father's Austin A40, a rather splendid car and the one on which I later learnt to drive as part of our household and, therefore, not an indigent part of Hong Kong life. The third was to ride the ding-dings.

Ding-dings was the colloquial name for the trams that ran from Kennedy Town in the west through the city's centre (Central) to the eastern extremity at Shau Kei Wan. A branch line went around the racecourse and sports ground at Happy Valley; originally, the only area of flat land in the Colony and so once covered in graves.

In 1949, the original single track was replaced with a double track to annoy motorists even more as they were not permitted to cross the tracks except at special points. My favourite vantage point was on the front seat of the upper deck (first class), cost 10 cents however long or short your journey. It cost five cents (third class) downstairs. The trams were slow and noisy but they travelled along the streets that represented the formation of Hong Kong itself from the Central area of European entrepreneurship to the further areas which were much more traditional Chinese.

The other mode of travel particularly in the centre and along the flat harbour areas was the rickshaw. This was a two-wheeled passenger cart with arms between which the rickshaw drawer pulled the cart. These were an extremely popular mode of cheap transport, particularly in the central area at rush hour when executives wished to get home or to the Star Ferry. Traffic jams were frequent and involved many Cantonese words of abuse from puller to puller. The pullers were considered to be at the very bottom of the social scale and were often poor immigrants seeking a living. Their only escape from reality was with opium, an abuse problem not just limited to rickshaw pullers. I found it very difficult to accept their poor position in life and, as a child often does, I just had to accept something that I could do nothing about.

When I was younger, the most striking building at the centre of European Hong Kong was the Hong Kong and Shanghai bank. A magnificent edifice; it dominated Statue Square. Oddly enough its main entrance was at the rear of the building facing the harbour and was guarded by bearded Sikh officers, armed and resplendent. They were aided either side of the entrance by two beautiful stone statues of lions. One was named Stephen and one Stitt, in honour of two past managers and their noses were often rubbed for good luck.

The Bank of China (left) built by Mao Tse Tung in 1952, just a
few stories higher than the Hong Kong and Shanghai Bank

Chapter 29

Statue Square was home to the cricket ground and club which itself was flanked by the Hong Kong Club, the Supreme Court and the Princes and Queens buildings. Within the square were the Cenotaph and the statue of the Queen, the square being divided by Des Voeux Road the main east-west artery.

Returning in 1951, the whole aspect of the square had changed with the addition to the east of the Hong Kong and Shanghai bank the structure of the Bank of China. Itself an architectural marvel built by the Communist Chinese, it stood 25 feet taller than its rival – just a way of showing unspoken superiority, I suppose.

Another most noticeable change was the adoption by the Chinese women of the cheongsam. This delightful mode of dress had been invented by the womenfolk of Shanghai but had been banned by the Communist regime. It flourished, however, in Hong Kong. The dresses were beautifully made in figure-hugging styles with the noticeable feature of slits up the side, often to the thigh. With high heels, a leather bag and white gloves, it particularly suited the grace of the Cantonese women and was worn by women of all social levels.

Another marked change, particularly in Central, was the integration of Europeans and Chinese and the westernisation of Chinese clothing in this business area. European men still wore suits and European women European clothes.

Travelling on my Ding-ding either east or west of the central area I would come to the traditional Chinese areas, one of the features of which were the 'ladder' streets. These narrow streets ran at right angles to the tram tracks and climbed up the steep hillside, often with steps between the tiny shops on each level.

Here was the true essence of Chinese life. The streets were crowded, all movement and noise, with conical hatted coolies both men and women bearing goods on bamboo poles, dogs stretched out or scavenging, old men on their chairs smoking or playing fan-tan or mah-jong or chatting or just watching life in the sun. Here the smells were of joss sticks, of tobacco with vague wafts of opium smoke, the sounds were of traders calling out their wares, of mah-jong tiles being slammed down, often of firecrackers to celebrate some occasion and over all this the sound from many radios of Chinese opera, discordant to the European ear, so perhaps, competing with each other. No one seemed to mind.

One of the two very popular means of inner city transport – the rickshaw

Chapter 30

Above the narrow streets, bamboo poles or ropes were slung between each rooftop supporting laundry or songbirds, or chickens or all three with pots of jasmine or bougainvillea, hanging down to perfume the walls.

Amongst the shops, selling just about everything you could imagine would be those selling noodles or won ton or soups or dim sum. A choice of wonderful snacks for a curious child.

Sometimes, my mother would take me, as a treat, over to Kowloon to Hong Kong's premier hotel, the Peninsula, for tea. Tea here was a classic tradition – finger sandwiches, cakes, choice of teas, all served to the strings of a chamber orchestra.

You felt you could have been in the Ritz in London despite the cutely capped Chinese messenger boys who walked through the lounge with a bell and board calling for some guest required on the telephone.

After tea, we would walk around Nathan Road, the main artery at this side of the harbour where the atmosphere seemed to be quite different.

In the side streets you would find more tourist attractions, more street food sellers know as *dai pai dongs*, less emphasis on European business. There seemed to be more awareness of those who were fleeing Communist China at the rate of 3000 refugees a day, meaning more beggars, more police presence and more evidence of the squatter villages that were growing up around the outskirts of Kowloon.

However, the similarity, on both sides of the harbour was that the Europeans were few and the Chinese many. It was just as well that there seemed, even to me as a child, a precocious one perhaps, a mutual understanding that life was survival and you accepted that each could benefit the other. Fantasy perhaps but I am not too sure.

The famous Star Ferry – still running today

Chapter 31

From just about everywhere in the harbour, you could look at the island and see an exquisite white pagoda. My curiosity had to be satisfied, so my mother took me to the Tiger Balm Gardens in which the pagoda stood so proudly. This proved to be no ordinary garden. Created in the 1930s by the inventor of Tiger Balm, a Chinese cure-all balm, he built his opulent home and in a series of caves and grottos he created tableaux. I wondered if he had been brought up on Grimm's fairy tales or on Struwwelpeter for each tableaux was garish in the extreme, its life-size statues depicting scenes that could have been taken from Dante's Inferno. The only explanation my mother could give me was that the tableaux were intended as a warning to those who offended against society. To be honest, the why remains a mystery, but I quite enjoyed the horror and the strong impression they created.

All too soon, this holiday was over and I took the three-day flight back to school. Then, like my holidays, the four years at Worth Priory had flown by and I had succeeded gaining my admission to Downside Public School. Another chapter of my life was about to begin.

Downside Abbey had been created by Benedictine monks, originally from Douai in Flanders who, in 1814, settled at Mount Pleasant in the village of Downside in Somerset. The monastery was completed in 1876 and the Abbey church, a superb example of the Gothic revival style, was finally completed in 1938. Attached to the monastery was a small school for boys.

In the early 1900s, a monk, Dom Leander Ramsay, planned new buildings, two of which became the two sides of the main quadrangle. They were completed in 1912 and this development marked the foundation of the modern Downside school.

Before setting off on this new adventure, my mother and I flew back to England in BOAC's Comet jet airliner. This was extraordinary. The journey that had taken three days was now completed in one. We still stopped at various airports en-route but there was far less noise despite the four jets and the comfort had improved. This was 1953 and the terrible tragedies that effected the Comet did not happen until 1954. We were lucky as after seeing me off to school, my mother returned safely to Hong Kong again in one of the Comets.

Built in the extraordinary Tiger Balm gardens, the white pagoda
stands out against Hong Kong's hillside.

Chapter 32

On arrival in London, we stayed in the Onslow Court Hotel in South Kensington which was later to feature in my young life. My mother created a very pleasant tradition which she always maintained whenever she was in England and I was going back to school. The train would leave for school at about 3:30 in the afternoon, so at 12:30 we would enter Scott's restaurant, then in Leicester Square, sit up at the counter and I was allowed to enjoy half a lobster and a glass of Chablis wine. It was a shame that she was not often in England on my returns to school.

As pupils, we now swapped Victoria Station for Paddington Station and Crawley for Bath. From Bath, coaches took us to the village of Stratton on the Fosse where the entry gates to the school and main quadrangle were positioned.

The school was a somewhat lower elevation than the Abbey, so to get to the Abbey we would pass the communal lavatories known as the 'Gruesomes' or for some strange reason 'the yards', turn a corner and up a flight passing the dining rooms, both ours and the monks, along a corridor and up another flight to our entrance to the Abbey itself.

It was and is a magnificent structure. We entered and walked to the centre aisle. To our right was the choir where the monks sat and beyond them the altar. To the left, and on either side of the aisle, row after row of pews for the boys, some 600 of them, and at the rear seating for visitors. Beautiful as the abbey was inside, it was equally beautiful outside with its gothic structure and its commanding tower.

As new boys, fortunately, many of us friends from our four years at Worth, we settled into what appeared to be prefabricated huts. We were allocated lockers, I think mine was 288, but whatever number it was, it was to be my locker for the four years to come. Just to start us on the front foot, on our first evening, there was a bum inspection. We all lined up dropped our trousers and showed our rear ends to the inspecting housemaster. Lord alone knows what this was meant to achieve, but happily once done, our body parts remained sacrosanct for the next four years.

Chapter 33

The years at Worth were marked with gentleness and pleasure both in the way in which we were treated as boys and in the beauty of our surroundings.

My first impression of Downside was that I was now entering a new world moving towards adolescence and adulthood. The school was impressive. It seemed to be much larger than Worth and it felt as if my childhood was over and I was going to have to find different responses to this different world. Fortunately, I was going to share these preoccupations with about one hundred other new boys.

One of the first rumours that spread like wildfire was that our headmaster, Dom Wilfred Passmore, was a disciplinarian and a tyrant. It was said that pupils in a previous year had called a strike against conditions and assembled in the main square. It required only the presence of the headmaster coming out through the front door for the assembly to disperse in all directions. Strike over.

This did not concern me nor my fellow pupils too much as we were far more concerned with finding our way around and fitting in with the school's routines and we were only in junior school – not really the real thing!

The first thing we had to accommodate other than our surroundings and daily life was our religious duties. As in prep school, we attended three Low Masses per week and Low and High Mass on Sundays. Added to this, we had Compline, a lengthy sermon called Sodality, Vespers and Benediction. These were compulsory and meant that each Sunday we spent nearly three hours in the abbey.

In the abbey, us new boys sat in the front pews, the seniors and prefects at the back. A wonderful custom that impressed us was that when the first XV rugby team won, its members would wear a rose in their buttonhole and, at the end of High Mass, were the first to leave their pews at the back of the abbey and walk down the aisle silently admired by the rest of the school. (Four years later, I had the privilege of being one of them.)

The impressive façade of the abbey and tower of Downside Abbey

Chapter 34

High Mass was quite a spectacle, particularly, at celebrations such as Easter. First, boys in surplices would enter from the back of the abbey, carrying baskets of rose petals which they would scatter up the aisle. Then would come three thurifers. Thurifers were the incense carriers. They each carried a thurible, a censer with chains, attached to a ring at the top. Inside the censer was burning charcoal and the smouldering incense. Each thurifer would swing his thurible back and forth until he arrived at just before the choir stalls. Here, with a flick of the wrist, he would create a circle with the thurible and make a right-hand turn. It was quite impressive, particularly swinging the thurible with enough speed to keep the hot ashes in the censer. Then followed the cross-bearer and the monks, all in ceremonial robes, leading the abbot up to the choir and altar. Accompanied by Gregorian chant and the melodious organ music, the Mass would begin.

One of the annual religious events was a Retreat, held in the Easter term. A retreat lasted four days and three nights and was held by a Jesuit priest brought in for the occasion. The aim of a retreat was to provide us with the chance to 'contemplate God's role in our lives'. It was meant to enhance our spirituality. The four days consisted of lectures from the

Jesuit, question and answer sessions, spiritual readings, time for reflection, prayer sessions and benedictions.

One of my better subjects was history and as well as normal classes, we had history tutorials where interested students from different years gathered to increase their knowledge. I sat next to my senior by a couple of years, a boy called Auberon Waugh, son of Evelyn Waugh, the famous novelist. Auberon, like me, was an iconoclast but he was far better at it than I was. He also, like me, did not like the fire and brimstone style of Jesuit philosophy as thrust at us during these retreats.

He decided that if we could raise the anger of the Jesuit by continually asking him ludicrous questions, it was likely that he would throw us out of the class. We became very good at it and it usually only took ten to fifteen minutes until we were banned from the classroom and told to do penance by reading some religious tract until the end of that session. We could keep this up for days and learnt a lot more history by using our banishment for readings of our own choice.

The regularity of our life was dramatically interrupted in November 1955 when a fire that began in the gym burnt through the night and destroyed a further three prefabricated dormitories causing extensive damage over two acres. Auberon Waugh claimed in his autobiography 'Will this do?' that many people including his father believed that he might have been responsible for the fire. He neither denied nor admitted to it. He did, however, claim that he did invent a story about a group of monks rushing into the burning dormitories and rescuing forty boys. This he fed to the journalists and television crews at the gate gaining extensive coverage. The silver lining was that there were no lives lost and the insurance money paid for a smart new gym and improved, modern dormitories.

Chapter 35

As at Worth, I made friends, quite by accident, two of whom in particular were to be very useful to me. They were Arbuthnot and Carter. Michael Carter was the son of the school doctor. His family home was just to the West of the school. John Arbuthnot's family home, on the other hand, was just to the east of the school. Both had generous parents who happily supplied food and drink to growing boys and in Arbuthnot's case his parents supplied not only food and drink, but they had converted an outhouse into a teenagers' playground with soundproofing and gramophone records. As an added bonus, he also had a very attractive mother and sister.

Each day would start with 'assembly' which in turn, would start with prayers. This was attended by the whole school and, if memory serves, most of the lay masters. The headmaster would highlight any events of importance and off we would then go to breakfast and the morning lessons. Then lunch and the afternoon would be for sport, the sports grounds being some little distance away past the cricket grounds. Tea, more lessons, dinner and evening assembly. At this, the headmaster would read out the names of those boys whom he wished to see. This invariably meant boys who were to be punished. The rest of the evening would be for ourselves, either to catch up on lessons, listen to gramophone records or the radio or, more often than not, gossip or read.

Educationally, the routine was the same, the years divided into the three terms, my least favourite being the Easter term where we were introduced not only to hockey but to boxing – compulsory boxing too. I hated it and dreaded each Easter term when I had to get into a ring, in those days with no head guards, only mouth guards, and stand there to be hit by someone stronger and bigger than me. Made no sense at all and due to my incompetence and fear, eventually my name was withdrawn from the boxing schedule. It did take two years to achieve this relief.

Our schedule and lessons were created to prepare us for the two major examinations, the common entrance or O levels and the advanced examination or A levels. The first was general and involved usually about eight subjects. At the end of this and depending on which subjects you were more competent, you were streamed into the literate or into the mathematic programmes, the mathematic including physics and other subjects completely alien to me. I settled for the literate courses, English, Geography, French and History. I say I settled. There was no choice. I just ended up in them.

Chapter 36

Towards the end of your first year as a junior, you were allocated your senior house. There were four of them, Caverel, Barlow, Roberts and Smythe. I was allocated to Caverel, Housemaster Dom Aelred Watkin, where I would spend the next three years.

Looking back, I was extremely lucky in my allocated house and housemaster, Dom Aelred Watkin. His grandmother had been Italian which was our first emotional link, but he was decidedly idiosyncratic, another link. Stocky of figure and like me, inclined to clumsiness, he was blessed with a great sense of humour and an understanding that 'boys will be boys'. An attribute that most affected us as worshippers of female film stars was that he had once been a great friend of Deborah Kerr, then a recognised beauty and leading film actress. I always wondered if he became a monk through a failure to win her attentions, but probably not.

In our first year of senior school, we had to fag for one of the boys in their last year. This was not an arduous task. Boys in their last year had their own studies whereas we were still living in dormitories – dormitories that could be so cold in winter that the icicles formed on the inside of the windows. We were required to keep his study tidy, clean his shoes and army boots, run errands, but I don't remember any outlandish requests or anything that caused me discomfort.

We were controlled by both masters and prefects. For minor infringements we were punished by having to write lines on blue paper usually about 500. I learned a poem called 'Mullion in the Summer time' by A. P Herbert. I churned it out whenever required. I hope whoever punished me became heartily sick of it.

More serious infringements would mean a beating, either with a leather strap or a rattan cane either by the housemaster or, if very, serious by the headmaster. Six whacks was the minimum, twelve the maximum. The punisher would always shake your hand after each punishment. I suppose, to show good will. All you, as the recipient, wanted to do was to get as far away from him as possible to try and lessen the pain and allow in the worst cases for your tears to flow. You received them on your bare backside and I can assure my readers it was not a pleasant experience and one you hoped to avoid for most of your schooldays. That old adage that it never did me any harm may have some truth in it, but it was a damned unpleasant experience at the time.

Chapter 37

At the end of this first year, my father had returned to England for my and their summer holidays. My father who loved the South of England, in particular the coast, rented a house in a village near Lewes called Barcombe Mills and here my grandmother joined us. It was a very pretty house with a pond, gardens and was in striking distance to most of his favourite seaside towns, Brighton, Eastbourne and Hastings. My grandfather would join us for the odd Sunday, leaving his companion at home and it was curious to see the only two grandparents I had ever known to behave in such an English manner, in other words with good English manners. It was only when my grandfather returned to the station to go home that my grandmother in true Italian style would raise her eyes, eyebrows and hands in an expression of wonder that she had ever found such an Englishman to her taste.

Her bowel movements also amused me. Whenever it was time for the table to be cleared or washing up to be done, my grandmother said she had to go to the loo.

Surprisingly, if it was time for a treat, there seemed to be nothing wrong with her bowels at all.

These were the great years of the crooners. Amongst the men were Bing Crosby, Dean Martin, Pat Boone and Frank

Sinatra, amongst the females Peggy Lee, Doris Day and Rosemary Clooney but a new sound was being heard – the sound of skiffle, the sound being led by Lonnie Donegan. Big bands were still popular and some jazz musicians such as Chris Barber, but jazz was not mainstream.

In America, but unbeknown to us, musicians and singers were developing jazz and rhythm and blues. Breaking onto the scene was a singer called Elvis Presley, who was bringing a new and exciting sound to us, unlike anything we had ever heard before. The song we all wanted was called Hound Dog. I remember going into a record shop in Eastbourne and asking for the record to be told by the sales assistant that you don't want that rubbish, buy a nice Lonnie Donegan. I'm glad to say I did not take her advice.

This was my last holiday in England with both my parents and my grandmother. At the end of the summer, my grandmother returned to her companion in Rome and my father to Hong Kong. I returned to school wondering where I would be spending my holidays in England in the future, to whom would I be farmed out this time as the Podmores had retired from active duty.

Chapter 38

It was expected that at the end of our time at school we would be called up to do National Service – two years of our life before going to University or on to other occupations. To prepare us for a military life, we became members of the school's combined cadet force or Corps. We were issued with a proper uniform with Sam Browne belt, spats, boots that had to be polished until you could see your face in them and when issued for parade, a rifle. Once a week, we would spend a couple of hours in an afternoon being on parade where we were marched up and down and given orders to 'slope arms' and 'present arms', just like real soldiers. We even had platoons.

For further preparation, the army offered public school boys the opportunity to spend two weeks in the summer at a proper army camp. I have no idea whether this was meant to be compulsory, but for some reason, unknown to us, but for which we were grateful, the Downside authorities would not permit us to go to them.

Towards the end of our time at Downside, regular army officers came to the school to test our proficiency in the ways of the military world. One of my examinations stands out in my memory. I was being examined on my skill at firing a Bren gun, a type of machine gun. I was spread eagled on the ground with the gun in front of me pointing at some distant target. The officer began his inquisition by asking me whether I played cricket. On saying yes, he asked me in which position did I play. I told him that I was a wicket keeper and an opening batsman. "Bloody good show," he replied. "Carry on. You've passed. I'll see you at Sandhurst." It is just as well he didn't ask me in which team I played. It was certainly not one of the better ones.

I am not sure when we heard that National Service was to be abolished. Any English male born after September 1939 would not have to serve. Obviously, this included me and nearly all my friends, but we continued with our military training until we left the school.

Rationing for nearly everything was abolished in July 1954. Even in the days of comprehensive rationing, there was a priority for food for children and, therefore, we did not suffer either at Worth or at Downside. We were well fed with three weekly highlights. On Monday, Wednesday and Friday, bread was freshly baked in the school's ovens. The wonderful smell of baking bread wafted through the school's corridors making our mouths salivate in anticipation. The taste was as good as the smell, augmented with a generous slice of butter.

Chapter 39

To supplement our diet, we had a school tuck shop laden with sweets and chocolates in which to spend our weekly pocket money.

I befriended, Tom, who ran the shop. He was a retired Police Officer having worked at Scotland Yard and, from time to time, he would tell us about the Black Museum (now called the Crime Museum) and the extraordinary collection of crime artefacts therein. You can imagine our excitement when he told us that he had arranged for me and three of my friends to visit the museum during our next holiday.

Co-incidentally, a famous series called 'The Black Museum', narrated by Orson Welles was a regular feature on Radio Luxembourg having being first aired there in 1953. It was compulsive listening, each episode featuring the story of a murder, the vital clue to its solving being housed in the museum. We were now going to visit this unique museum which was only available to police officers and not, in those days, to the general public.

The museum was housed in the basement of Old Scotland Yard. Its rooms had bare stone walls, showing marks of flooding in earlier times and smelling slightly of damp or mildew. Each room was lit by a single naked bulb, hanging from the dark ceilings. Every aspect added to the effect of a chamber of horrors which it was as it housed the items that led to the arrest of murderers and general villains as well as examples of the methods of the murders. It was seriously gruesome, but absolutely fascinating to our teenage minds.

The tour took about half an hour, followed by a visit to Scotland's Yard more brightly lit cafeteria where we were treated to tea and cakes. They didn't taste quite as good as normally!

Christmas of my first year at Senior School was spent in London with my mother at the Onslow Court Hotel, Queensgate, in South Kensington, one of the popular middle-class residential areas. The hotel was well situated in the heart of South Kensington, near bus routes, the underground and a collection of museums. The hotel was, however, decidedly old fashioned. It was owned by a Quaker family and therefore was a temperance hotel with no bar and no service of alcohol. However, the restaurant manager, Mr Mario, who had been there for at least 10 years, kept a stock of wine which you could buy from him when required.

Chapter 40

My room was a single with a basin, bed, wardrobe and armchair with a slightly grimy window, lace curtained, that looked out over Old Brompton Road. The lavatory and bathrooms were shared and were along the corridor. The hotel was recognised not only as a hotel for visitors but also as a home for more elderly, mostly retired gentlefolk of moderate means who lived there permanently.

Amongst them was a younger man, John Paramore, in his late '40s, who had been a ballet dancer but who had inherited enough money to retire and to take up permanent residence in the hotel. He had already spent ten years in the hotel and like the other permanent guest, qualified for his own table. He became a great friend of my mother as he was probably the only person there close to her own age.

What the hotel did have, I am not sure whether by popular request, was a television lounge. There was only one channel, the BBC, and programmes were only broadcast in black and white and only in the evenings. Despite these limitations, it was a thing of great wonder to us, hugely enjoyable and it became an evening ritual to watch.

The other advantage of the television lounge was that it was dark. Dorothy was a young girl, the same age as me, who was staying with her parents in the hotel. We had for some time been looking in a friendly manner at each other whenever the chance arose. It arose when we found ourselves the only two in the lounge and sitting next to each other – by design, I hasten to add. This was my glorious first kiss. And it was so pleasant, so nerve tingling, so delicious that we kept at it until someone else entered the lounge. My very first girlfriend, my very first kiss.

During the following week before she and her parents left the hotel, we found every opportunity to resume this delightful activity even going so far as to explore each other a little further through the barrier of our clothes. It was all over far too soon, but never to be forgotten.

This new 'me' seemed to appeal to other women. There was a delightful Irish waitress, extremely well endowed, who waited on me at my table. Having paid me virtually no attention, she began to show an interest in the new me. She invited me out to a dance at the Hammersmith Palais, then one of London's leading dance halls featuring the Joe Loss band and popular singers. Off we went and danced the night away. We returned to the hotel for me to receive a hug, kiss and squeeze at the door to her quarters.

Chapter 41

One early evening, she invited me up to her room to wait for her to get dressed for our evening out. This, I thought, was going to be the next step in my learning curve. My expectation knew no bounds when she stripped off her shirt and paraded around in her bra, showing off her voluptuous chest. Then I realised, this parade was at her window and was for the advantage of some burly builders working on the building opposite who were reciprocating her interest. I hoped my disappointment didn't show, but I realised that I was not yet up to her league. We went to the dance and said goodbye.

What I had not realised was that at the end of this holiday, my mother was to return to Hong Kong. She explained that both she and my father thought me old enough now that I did not need to be farmed out and that, henceforth, I would spend my holidays when in England here in the Onslow Court Hotel. John Paramore would keep his eye on me with help and advice when needed.

You cannot imagine my astonishment, trepidation, fear, confusion and I must admit some element of pride that, at fifteen, I was to be given such a responsibility as looking after myself. I also had to admit I felt a sense of superiority over my school friends who had only families to go home to.

I also felt that as I was quite used to being without parents for months at a time, sometime for a year, this new adventure would mean more to me than missing them. On reflection, this must have been a strange and difficult decision for them but I can only assume they thought it was best for me and for them. We only ever discussed it again once. To my shame and my only excuse can be that I was going through a rebellious teenager period, but I once tore into my mother for deserting me and for leaving me to fend for myself. I reduced her to tears about which I am not proud and only wish that I might have, at least, later begged her forgiveness.

Fortunately, one of my close school friends, John Burns, also lived in London, reasonably close by. His parents were charming, ex-military couple who had an apartment in Carlton Terrace, a very smart street near Trafalgar Square and the West End. During the holidays we spent a lot of time together, playing at being young men about town. We would visit Jules Bar in Jermyn Street for cocktails, Fortnum and Mason's for tea and the manikin show and the new West End coffee bars to try and pick up girls – unsuccessfully, I might add. But, often, if on my own, I would spend much of the day in cinemas – often seeing three movies in one day starting at midday and sometimes seeing two films in one cinema or moving about the cinemas in Leicester Square and around Piccadilly.

Chapter 42

In the evening, more often than not, I would have dinner at, now, my own table and then walk round the corner to the Denmark Pub for a couple of pints with John Paramore who became a very great friend in these strange times.

I can't remember when I first had a cigarette. When we lived in Corfe Castle, I do remember my first drag of a friend's Woodbine amongst the wild garlic on the slopes of the castle. I must have been around ten years old, I suppose. I was certainly smoking cigarettes whilst at Downside. Our bathrooms were at the very top of the school with dormer windows. I certainly remember lighting up after a bath and blowing the smoke out of the window. It is only now that I realise that the smell of smoke would have clung to me and would not have fooled a master or prefect that might have come by. In my last year, we were allowed to smoke in one room reserved for those addicted to the habit.

Certainly, I was a confirmed smoker once I left school as all my film star heroes and heroines smoked as well as virtually everyone around me. Oddly enough, not my parents, but cigarettes were an almost a necessity to offer at any social occasion.

I suppose, I was about 14 when I realised that from my normal seat at the back of the classroom, I was having difficulty seeing the blackboard clearly. Once it was confirmed that I needed spectacles, I was sent to an optician in Bath. Bath was the centre of all pleasure to us schoolboys. It was our local big city full of shops that sold teas and cigarettes and magazines and there was a cinema, but it was not often that we could find an excuse to go there.

I decided that my teeth needed looking at least once a term and that my eyesight should also be checked at least once a term but not at the same time. This meant a minimum of two visits each term and, if you timed it correctly, you took the early bus in, had an early appointment and then were free to go to the first showing at the cinema where you sat back to enjoy the film and the cigarettes that you had sensibly purchased beforehand. After tea in a café near the bus stop, you took the late bus back. Wonderful.

Chapter 43

Though, I say it myself, I was not handsome, but I wasn't bad looking, so I was surprised when an elderly man made an advance at me. It only happened twice and twice in the Bath cinema. It is a strange experience and one you are not expecting. Well, certainly not the first time. I was sitting minding my own business, watching the movie when a man moved onto the seat next to me. Next thing I knew, he had put his hand high up on my thigh. My first reaction was shock. What on earth was he doing? This was just so unexpected. It took me a second or two to realise what he was up to. Once I realised what it was all about, I had the audacity to turn to him and say if he didn't move off I would hit him. He rose and left immediately.

When it happened the second time, I was prepared and immediately threatened the same punishment with the same immediate result. Neither, though over quickly, were pleasant experiences.

One of the advantages, or disadvantages depending on how you look at it, is at an all-boys school there are no girls so the opportunity for sports or hobbies are almost endless.

My preferences were for amateur dramatics, usually cast as a girl, stamp collecting, model railways (Hornby Double O and Triang) as well as writing scurrilous songs and poems and writing very bad short stories. One very satisfying advantage of being involved in amateur dramatics was that each year we were invited to take part, or parts, in the Bath Festival. Often, we would do excerpts from Shakespeare, one of my star roles being the porter in *Macbeth,* 'Here's a knocking indeed' or reading from a passage that we had not seen before. I was quite good at this which was to stand me in good stead in later life.

These trips were, of course, another reason to come into Bath, the big city and to enjoy all its pleasures.

I have said that there were no girls at Downside. That is true, but there were young women. They were the Spanish girls who worked as waitresses in our dining room. Over time, I became quite friendly with one of them and often made her laugh by trying to ask her for things in Spanish, of which I spoke not a word.

Chapter 44

With extraordinary boldness, I asked her one day if she would like to meet me, can you believe, behind the cricket pavilion. Much to my surprise she agreed and we made our tryst. It was a particularly cold night on which we met and to keep warm we entered into a strong, passionate clinch which progressed into a certain amount of physical exploration through our clothes.

Just as it was getting interesting, a torch was shone in our faces and we were arrested by a master. I do not know nor was I ever told what happened to the poor girl, but I was taken to the headmaster and given six of the best and threatened with expulsion if I ever misbehaved in this way again. I am pretty sure to this day that I was told on by one of my not close friends who was jealous that I had succeeded in chatting up this poor girl. But I will never know.

My sixteenth birthday was another landmark. I was given a Vespa scooter. This increased my freedom no end. These were the days of the Mods and the Rockers, two competing tribes who eventually ended up in a pitched battle on the front at Brighton. The Rockers were the motor cycle lads, with Brylcreemed hair, jeans, leather jackets and winkle picker shoes. The Mods were the scooter brigade riding their

Lambrettas and Vespas. Their style of dress was more modern, more Carnaby Street, more stylish with coiffured hair and branded shoes. I, of course, got it all wrong. I wore jeans, a leather jacket and the Brylcreemed hair (thank you, Denis Compton, a cricketer hero of the day who advertised the product) and rode my Vespa.

Fortunately, my scooter had a home during term times at the house of a friend near Downside so any chance of me meeting up with unfriendly Rockers was severely limited. But it was terrific fun driving up and down from London to school in the days before the M5 was built and to drive to see my friends out of London during the holidays.

After one particular holiday at home in Hong Kong, I was flying back to England for the winter term. The conditions must have been quite right as I looked out of the window of my 377 Stratocruiser, I was fascinated by a sight I have never forgotten. It was night and the moon was full. As we flew along the moon seemed to fly along with us and as I looked down it seemed to be flying along the ground, picking out the rice fields, pagodas, temples and villages of the Thai countryside over which we were flying. It was quite magical and I have never experienced it again.

Chapter 45

This particular flight gave me another unforgettable moment. We were approaching Cairo when the Captain advised over the intercom that he had a problem. The outer starboard engine had developed a fire which they were unable to extinguish. We were not to worry as he had an alternative to cure the problem. This was to go into a dive – a recognised method to resolve this particular problem. We should, therefore, strap ourselves in whilst he carried out the manoeuvre.

Strapped in, but obviously to calm our nerves, they put on the background music. Pat Boone, at that time, was a seriously popular crooner whose specialty was modernising religious and spiritual songs. His voice came through with the first line of one of his greatest hits – *Closer God I am to Thee*. Hugely appropriate in the circumstances but, fortunately, not applicable as I am still here to tell the tale.

It was very near the end of my last Easter term at Downside, spring 1958 and I was coming up to 18 in July. A summons came from Dom Passmore, the headmaster that I was to attend his study at 6:00 pm – the caning hour. Wondering what I had done now and how serious could it be to be summoned in such a manner to his office. I duly attended in some trepidation at 6:00 pm.

"Come in, Peter, sit down." This seemed friendly enough. "I have to congratulate you. You have somehow managed to achieve a place at university in September. You have been accepted by an Oxford College but there is a problem. As you do not have to do National Service, you must wait two years before you can take up your place at Oxford as the National Service boys have priority."

"You can however accept an offer made by the third member of the three Trinity Universities, Trinity College in Dublin where you can take up your place in September."

"What would you like to do?"

I didn't need time to think as I had no intention of hanging around for two years, so I told him that I would take the place in Dublin.

Chapter 46

"Excellent," he continued. "There is more. You have played 1st XV rugby for the school. But, let us be honest. You are hopeless at cricket. I can see no point in you really wasting your time further here. I have spoken to your parents and we have agreed that you should go home to Hong Kong until September. I understand you are to travel home by an Italian liner, but your housemaster will have the details. So, I suggest you pack your bags and say your farewells. Neither your housemaster nor I have any idea of what may become of you but you do have some sort of charm and quite an engaging personality so I wish you every success."

He stood up from behind his desk, came around to shake my hand and clapped me on the shoulder.

Stunned, but delighted I left his office, visibly shaking. It was over. Eight years of Benedictine education and life at school had ended and I was free to enjoy at least four months at home in Hong Kong.

The week flew by with some regrets, I must admit, but the following Monday found me at Heathrow, now unrecognizable from the days of the tented marquees only some six years before, ready to board a BEA flight to Rome to stay with my grandmother for a few days until I was to board my ocean-going liner to Hong Kong.

Despite being a quarter Italian, I have never had much grasp of the language. This can cause complications. When I arrived at the exit gate at Rome's airport, there was an officious officer who told me that I should have a different exit pass. I replied in my best Italian, *"Perche? E stupido. Io ho questo."* What I didn't realise that in Italian 'E' can mean you or it. I meant it. He thought I was calling him stupid. His face went purple and he was about to arrest me when my grandmother who had been waiting for me at the exit pitched in. I have no idea what she said, but it must have been effective as I was eventually waved through. Another lesson learnt.

My grandmother lived with her partner, Tulio, a gentle man, who had recently retired from a lifetime of service on the Italian railway. They lived in an apartment in an area of Rome called the 'Secondo Parioli', conveniently situated only fifteen minutes by bus away from the Via Veneto, the thriving centre of social life in the 1950s.

Chapter 47

In Rome, also lived one of my school friends, John von Pflugel. John, in his holidays, worked at the Vatican radio and asked me if I would like to join him there one day. I, of course, agreed and I arrived at the Vatican to be shown through by a Swiss Guard to where John was waiting for me, before climbing the hill up to the radio station situated at the summit.

As we walked up the hill, which was traversed by paths and flower borders, a man in white robes was walking along one of the paths towards us. "Would you like to meet the Pope?" asked John. Even I could accept that this would be an exceptional honour to be given an opportunity to meet the Pope in private on the hills of his earthly home. The Pope was Pius XII. It is etiquette to kiss the Pope's Papal ring on his finger when meeting him which we did. He then asked me about myself, how I had enjoyed Downside and, with a twinkle, life with the Benedictines. After a little more social talk, he gave us his blessing and carried on his walk of meditation. Not everyone, Catholic or not, gets to meet the Pope in this way and it remains an unforgettable memory.

On the appointed day, my grandmother packed me up. I said my farewells to Tulio and to John and set off with my grandmother who was to accompany me from Rome to Naples where I was to board my passage to Hong Kong.

The liner was the MV Victoria, a recently built ocean-going steam ship, owned and run by an Italian company, Lloyd Triestino. It was a beautiful vessel with a carved superstructure, streamlined funnel and terraced after-decks that featured a pool and lido, one for each of the two classes of passengers. Its complement was for 286 first class passengers and 181 tourist passengers – a far cry from my last eastbound sea journey on the old SS Cynthia.

Within the vessel, which was centrally air-conditioned, were modern self-contained cabins, bar, restaurant, veranda, lounge, card room and reading room for both passenger classes. On deck, as well as the verandas and pools, there were areas for deck games, table tennis and at the stern of the vessel shot guns and equipment for skeet shooting.

Thanks to my father's generosity, I was shown by my smartly dressed Italian steward to my first-class cabin.

A wonderful way to travel home – the MV Victoria, one of Lloyd Triestinos modern fleet

Chapter 48

Adjacent to my cabin, there was a lady with two young children returning to Hong Kong to join her husband who had recently been transferred there to work in the Legal Service. Her name was Betty and her children were Miranda, aged eight and William, aged four. Miranda was an attractive, leggy young girl whose main occupation seemed to be knowing what her younger brother was up to and trying to keep him out of mischief. William, as I soon discovered, was a blond, blue eyed, adventurous and mischievous little boy, but he was not a keen eater.

He and I struck up a friendship which included me taking him up to the dining room and convincing him to eat by playing aircraft. I would put a piece of food on a fork and to the noise of a revving aircraft, the fork would rise from the plate and head for his mouth which would, with luck, open. Nine times out of ten, this method would work until after a week or so, he found eating a pleasure which he could undertake on his own.

William was also the cause of a lasting friendship between Betty and myself.

One day, I was lazing by the pool to hear a piercing scream from Betty who realised that William had fallen into the pool and was close to drowning. Both, Betty and I jumped into the pool, caught hold of William and heaved him up to the side of the pool. Fortunately, he had not swallowed too much water as we had managed to get to him in enough time.

Thereafter, I would usually join her gang, mainly made up of ex Pats from India, Singapore or Hong Kong, for drinks at the bar, have dinner at her table and generally socialise with those of her age which was everyone – except me.

It was also the start of a life-long love affair with gin and tonic and the opposite to the latest Italian hit song *Nel blu dipinto di blu, (Volare)* sung by Italy's premier crooner, Domenica Modugno, and played constantly by the Italian crew.

Daily life on the Victoria was nothing if not extremely pleasant. Life at sea began with breakfast, then the pool or deck games or table tennis or skeet shooting from the stern of the boat.

Chapter 49

Served by resplendent white coated Italian waiters and cooked by Italian chefs, lunch featured meals that you would be at home with in first class Italian restaurants. The afternoon might be a repeat of the morning with the addition that the serious bridge players would gather for an afternoon of cards. At around six, the passengers would retire to their cabins for showers and to dress for cocktails and dinner. Men changed into evening dress, usually white evening jacket, black tie and matching black trousers with patent leather shoes. The women wore their jewellery and long evening dresses.

After dinner, another Italian extravaganza, the bridge players might start again, dancing might begin and the drinking continue. Ships' officers would often join in for the dancing, but did not try to compete with the passengers in the consumption of alcohol.

This was the life of the colonials encapsulated into one long party.

Life on board would be interrupted at regular intervals when the liner docked, usually for two or three days, at the ports along our route.

Here was the chance for those who had lived previously at ports along the route to disembark for a few days to visit friends or relatives.

For me, it was a chance to visit ports and towns that I had only passed, almost in a dream, ten years previously.

Amongst those we visited, I particularly remember Bombay (now Mumbai), with its magnificent monument, the Gateway to India, and close by the splendour of the Taj Hotel. Then Colombo in Ceylon (Sri Lanka) where we took a trip along the coast to the old colonial fort of Galle, but the memory of most effect was our stop at Singapore.

Here, Betty went up country to visit some old friends for an overnight stay and I had the pleasure of Miranda and William's company for twenty-four hours. The learning curve is both strange and immediate when you experience the difference between a short period and a twenty-four-hour period of childcare – an enjoyable lesson though!

Chapter 50

It was also here that on a previous day, one of my companions who had worked in the Naval Dockyards took me to visit them and then on to see the infamous Changi Prisoner of war camp, notorious for the appalling conditions there. It is the place where the novel *King Rat* by James Clavell is set and, of course, the prison from which men were sent to work on the bridge over the River Kwai and the Sandahan Airfield.

Memories indelibly printed.

The closest in age to me was an attractive young woman on her way to 'take up a post' she explained, in Bombay, in India. My knowledge of courting had been confined to my school day adventure and my two London hotel episodes – not a wide base of experience.

Sunsets in the Indian Ocean can be magical and very romantic. In those days, the ocean at night would be alive with phosphorescence in and around the boat, particularly in its wake and above, with no light interference, the twinkling sea was matched by the twinkling stars. It was not only romantic but unforgettable.

This young lady and I, as we were approaching India, would after an evening at the bar, walk down to the stern of the boat to enjoy nature's magnificence. Leaning on the railing and washed by the light of the moon, it seemed only natural to enter into a clinch and enjoy some serious kissing.

Unfortunately, three factors arose that kept our passion from progressing. One was her refusal to progress further, the second was that we were only two nights out of Bombay and the third was her explanation that she was not going out to 'take up a post' but she was actually on her way to meet her husband. This was a serious disappointment as she was extremely attractive and I would have been honoured to have lost my virginity to her. Ah well! I would just have to keep going.

Chapter 51

It was not long after leaving Singapore that we steamed through the entrance between Sam Ka Tsuen and Sai Wan Shan into Hong Kong harbour and settled at out berth. My father and mother rushed on to meet me. My father was slightly taken aback that once we had shaken hands and made happy greeting noises, he was approached by the purser who presented him with a rather extensive invoice for my three weeks on-board. Despite an eyebrow lifted and a long glance in my direction, the account was settled and having introduced my parents to my now best friends in particular, Betty and her children, we disembarked, picked up my luggage and set off for home.

Though, I had been home for various summer holidays, only one was memorable, 1955 – unfortunately for the wrong reasons. The day after I arrived home, it was a beautiful day with a reasonable breeze blowing – the perfect day for a sail around the harbour. I telephoned Ah Ling to get the yacht ready and off we sailed, the breeze filling our sails and sending us along at a fair old pace. As we approached Kowloon, I asked Ah Ling, who was sitting at the top of the companionway, if I could make it round the buoy that I had never seen before. "Yes, okay go," he replied. I swung about and after a few metres and at full tilt, we came to a resounding and immediate stop. Ah Ling disappeared down the companionway arse over tit.

What I didn't know and I assume Ah Ling did not know either was that the buoy marked the end of the underwater foundations for the new runway that was being built out from Kai Tak Airport into the harbour. We had hit solid concrete. We managed to get the sails down and float away, raise the sails and struggle back to the yacht club.

I was woken the next morning by my mother, my father having left for his office, with the news that Ah Ling had been up all night bailing the water out of the yacht and he believed that we had split the hull. This proved to be true and I spent the rest of the holiday not only with no yacht which had been sent for repairs, but also suffering from my father's serious displeasure. I had left it to my mother to tell him the bad news.

Pause for a brief history lesson.

When we first arrived in Hong Kong in the late 1940s, the population was 600,000, spread over the islands, Kowloon and the new territories. When I returned for my extended holiday in 1958, it had exploded to 2.2 million and was growing daily.

Our yacht, a member of the Princess class, under power in
the harbour

Chapter 52

The civil war in China ended in 1949, with the victory won by Mao Zedong (Mao Tse Tung) and his Communist party. This led first to emigration from nearby China of agriculturists and poorer workers, followed by entrepreneurs and businessmen mainly from Shanghai. It also included members of the 'triads', the criminal society that caused a certain amount of havoc for some years, particularly in Kowloon and Wan Chai.

Mao faced international embargos, so realised that if he left Hong Kong as a British Colony, he could use it not only to gain foreign currency from supplying food and water to the Colony, but also using it for trade. He ordered his army to stop advancing at Sham-Chun and the border was set up there as the extent of the new territories. To show his intent, The Bank of China was opened in 1951, next to and taller than the Hong Kong and Shanghai bank.

This mass immigration had both advantages and disadvantages. There was suddenly, something that Hong Kong had never had before, entrepreneurial expertise in manufacturing and a massive, cheap labour force. This in turn, led to massive slums, hillside encampments and even shacks set up on roofs.

A terrible fire in 1953 burnt down a whole shanty town in Shek Kip Mei, making 53,000 people homeless. This caused the government, under the governorship of Sir Alexander Grantham, to set about creating new towns, one in east Kowloon called Kwun Tong and one in the new territories called Tsuen Wan as well as the introduction of high rises to accommodate the bourgeoning population. Fortunes were beginning to be made.

The urban area, known as Central, continued to be relatively small, developed around the city of Victoria as well in part on the opposite shore of Kowloon.

A noticeable feature of my return was a relaxation from any semblance of apartheid. Rather than race, particularly in public transport, discrimination was noticeable only on the grounds of preference or wealth. On public transport and on the Star Ferry, the lower floor still cost five cents, the upper 10 cents, but the choice was yours.

This was the Hong Kong to which I returned in 1958.

The first thing to take place, other than a quick trip on the Peak Tram, was a family meeting about what to do with me.

Chapter 53

I had decided that I would like to be a journalist, so my parents arranged for me to go to a secretarial school in Wan Chai. A friend of my mother who was involved with Radio Hong Kong thought that I might be of use to the then Programme Producer, Ted Thomas.

I duly went down to meet him and I was sent into a studio to do a sound test. The studios were pretty basic. I sat at a desk on which was the microphone, handed headphones and facing me was a window in which the sound engineer, who doubled as my director, sat. I was given a news item to read and I gave inward thanks to those years of sight-reading at school. I was told to read straight off and I was going along quite well till I saw the lines 'and now we will play the Bumble Bee by Rimsky-Korsakov'. I swallowed hard and made it through without falling into the trap of saying Rimsky Corsets off.

I returned to Ted's office to be told that I had passed the test and that he would like me to carry out interviews for one of his programmes called 'In Hong Kong This Week'.

In those days, radio technology was nothing like it is nowadays. To record an outside interview, we had a microphone attached to a recorder, attached to a battery pack. It was cumbersome, heavy and a serious burden to carry around in Hong Kong's summer heat. Further, there was no Google. When told who I was to interview, I would have to search around through press cuttings to find out something about the person and what to talk about.

Once back in the studio and with the engineer, the recording was transferred to a large Ampex machine and we would edit the tape to the length required for the programme. At least, this gave one the opportunity to get rid of silences and mistakes.

Three interviews stand out in my memory.

The first was the worst and the most difficult.

Chapter 54

Fortunately, it was in the studio, so no wearisome battery pack. However, I was to interview a young mainland Chinese girl, a brilliant violinist who had won an entrance to a music competition in America. Unfortunately, she knew only about five words of English and my Mandarin was nil. You can well imagine the difficulty with trying to get five minutes of conversation onto tape. We managed by me leading with questions about violin playing or music competitions or America and she replying yes.

It is not often that I was complimented by my boss, but this was once.

The second was wonderful. The famous basketball team, the Harlem Globe Trotters, who are still touring, were giving exhibition matches in town and I was sent to interview their captain. Having watched a game where basketball and comedy were extremely well mixed, in particular letting the much smaller Chinese team run through their legs, I came to interview the captain. I am five foot ten, he must have been six foot seven.

I would ask a question into the microphone at my height then have to reach up at arm's length to get his answer. Up and down the microphone went until we both burst out laughing. It was a wonderful interview with a truly delightful man.

The last interview in my memory was quite different. Being filmed in Hong Kong was a melodrama called *Ferry to Hong Kong*, starring Kurt Jurgens, Orson Welles and Sylvia Syms. I was sent to the Peninsula Hotel to interview Kurt Jurgens. My appointment was for 11 am.

I arrived at his suite on time to have my hand shaken and to be greeted by the comment that there was no point starting an interview until we had had a drink. We had one, then another, and then he suggested that we had lunch before starting. We managed to down a couple of bottles of wine over lunch and carried on drinking.

He was a very amusing raconteur, but at great length he told me how he despised Orson Welles. Welles had been a film hero of mine particularly after *The Third Man* but some years later having seen this melodramatic film which was pretty rubbishy, I think I came to agree with Kurt Jurgens. Welles was not invincible and could make serious mistakes.

Chapter 55

I had no alternative, but to abandon the interview, carry on drinking and make an appointment for the next day.

As I became more involved with Radio Hong Kong, I began to be called in to read the morning news if one of the regular newsreaders was ill or incapacitated. I enjoyed this immensely.

The programme would start off with a clip from a song from *Singing in the Rain*. 'Good morning, good morning. We danced the whole night through' and I was cued to start. "Good morning. I am Peter Hunt, the time is eight am and here is today's news."

What I did not realise that this exposure on the radio made you something of a celebrity. This struck home when one day I went over to a party at a block of flats in Repulse Bay. I knocked on the apartment door, was let in and started on a kindly proffered gin and tonic. After about ten minutes the host came up to me and asked me who I was. I had gone to the wrong apartment but on saying I was Peter Hunt, I was treated like an honoured guest and introduced to everyone. It proved to be a good party to get me in the right mood before changing apartments and attending the party to which I had actually been invited.

Concurrently, I began my schooling in the mysteries of typing and short hand, mysteries which, I hasten to add, I never conquered. Life was getting far too interesting.

I was the only 17-year-old boy in a class of 8, the other seven being young European women. One of them, very definitely, caught my eye and this immediate attraction seemed to be reciprocated. I soon discovered that her name was Valerie and she was the daughter of military parents who lived in the military compound at Magazine Gap.

A standard day for me would begin with taking the peak tram down to the terminus and a tram to Wan Chai where the secretarial school was held. Before entering the school, I would pop into the next-door barber and have a shave and a gossip. After school, I would catch a taxi, rickshaw or tram to the premises of Radio Hong Kong where I would find out if I was needed or to edit something I may have recorded the day before.

If not needed, the day was now my own.

Chapter 56

My parents were not heavy socialisers. My father always claimed that of the three senior partners in his firm, who were himself and the two other senior partners, appropriately named Profit and Black, it was he that did all the work and they did all the socialising.

Unless there was a specific function to go to or an occasional dinner party at home, my parents preferred to spend their evenings quietly at home. This was not for me and I began to spend more and more evenings with Betty and her husband, Everard, and their lively circle of friends. It was at one of these evenings that Betty said to me that her elder daughter Annabel, then about 13, coming up 14, was coming out from school in England for her summer holidays. She was convinced that if the two of us met, there would be trouble. I merely thought she was being quirky but in the event she was to prove spectacularly farsighted.

I did, in fact, meet Annabel that summer on the beach at Repulse Bay. Even as a mid-teenager, she was an exceptionally good-looking girl with a very good figure and a beautiful smile. However, her most attractive feature was that when she was talking to you, she made you feel that you were the centre of her attention – an attribute that many people should learn, but it just came to her naturally. To be fair, I couldn't understand Betty's premonition as I was pretty sure that, other than seeing her around and about for the rest of her holiday, I didn't expect to see her again. But that is, as they say, another story.

Up until 1956, European food was served either at home, in the hotels or clubs or in specifically European coffee shops such as the Dairy Farm. Virtually every restaurant sold Chinese food in one form or another and all street food was Chinese.

One style of Chinese restaurants developed after the Second World War became a major tourist attraction. They were the floating seafood restaurants in Aberdeen harbour. They were built in the style of palaces with inboard fish tanks from which you chose the fish you wished, which was then cooked and served. The two I remember were the Sea Palace and the Tai Pak. I think there was a third, but I no longer remember its name. To reach them, you boarded a sampan and were oared to and from the restaurants. It was all rather romantic with the added bonus that the food was excellent.

Chapter 57

In 1956, Maxim's was founded in Central. It was the first restaurant to introduce Western fine dining, splendid decor and live music. It was an immediate success particularly with the media, celebrities and business executives.

It became one of my favourite evening haunts.

Other than the LRC, the Yacht Club, the golf club and the Hong Kong club, all of which I had been a junior member for years and now a member, my favourite daytime haunt became the Foreign Correspondents Club.

Built on Conduit Road, it was a neo-Gothic building with a stately circular entrance porch reached by a set of circular steps. It had large rooms, a wide and expansive veranda with views over Central and across the harbour. Its heyday had been during the Korean War in the early 1950s. It was then the home, virtually, to the international press who telephoned their agents at the front and then wrote and sent back their stories from these luxurious and pleasant surroundings.

Here, lunch was preceded by their speciality a Gimlet, basically gin and lime juice, then followed by the best prawn curry on the island.

European society had developed into various tribes, the top two of which treated each other with condescension, but with the knowledge that they needed each other.

They were the government and the business community. The most powerful of the business community were known as the 'Hongs', the word having nothing to do with the word Hong Kong. It was the name given to the big business houses who had basically created Hong Kong – Jardine Matheson, Butterfield and Swire, Hutchinson and Wheelock Marden – Jardine, perhaps, being the greatest of them all.

During the '50s and into the early '60s, they were the masters of all they surveyed until the entrepreneurial Chinese businessmen began to outdo them in money, authority and power.

Chapter 58

What these business houses had managed to do was to reinvent themselves after the Korean War and the victory of Communism in China. Before that, Hong Kong had been an entrepôt concerned with sourcing goods and selling them on – tea and opium being the most famous. Now, with the influx of skilled manufacturers and entrepreneurs from Shanghai and other major Chinese cities, as well an enormous cheap labour force, Hong Kong became a manufacturing and export giant.

The government, headed by his excellency the Governor, included the Civil Service and the higher levels of the administration shared the top echelon with the business community. Supporting this level of society and a part of it were the legal, banking and service industries.

The third tribe was made up of the two military services most prevalent in Hong Kong, the Navy and the Army. Many of the codes of behaviour had been formulated by the officer class of the military and were based on status, schooling, regiment and what they described as good manners. An example of this was that only officers were allowed to be members of most of the clubs including the yacht club. One of my best friends was a squaddie doing his National Service in Hong Kong. I took him as my guest into the Yacht Club. Letters to the secretary followed complaining that a soldier, not an officer, had been invited in. The complainers, fortunately, were given short shrift in that society was changing and no longer being ruled by the dictates of the old school.

I witnessed two further examples of the old worldliness of the military tribe, a breed sadly no longer with us today.

The first was an example of the brash modernist against the traditional. My boss, Ted Thomas, had a very snazzy sports car. He was driving down to Central and looking for a parking space on the Peak Road. He saw a gap. He also saw a car, a Bentley, pull up in front of the gap with the intention of reversing in. He shot into the gap in his small car. Out of the Bentley came a uniformed general seething with anger. Ted wished him a good morning and started to walk away. The General shouted at him to come back immediately. Ted continued on his way at which the general shouted again to his departing back that his seconds would call on him later that day and that he should now consider himself challenged to a duel.

Chapter 59

The second was far more gentle. I was visiting my father's office in Central. It was pouring with rain. As I entered the lift, I was joined by Colonel Dowbiggin, an elderly army officer. He was beautifully dressed. He wore a jacket, waistcoat, shirt, tie and matching pocket-handkerchief. He sported a carnation in his buttonhole and on his feet his shoes sparkled and his spats were immaculate. To my surprise, however, he was wearing shorts. It looked so incongruous that I asked him if he realised that he was wearing shorts. "Stupid boy," he replied. "Don't you realise it's raining? Damned silly to go about getting one's trousers wet."

The final tribe included the rest – the non-officer class, those passing through particularly Australians and Americans and those who, for one reason or another, did not wish to be a part of this layered and, in part, snobbish society.

There was one place where the tribes and the Chinese congregated and intermingled. This was at the racetrack at Happy Valley. The Governor had his box, the Hongs had theirs, the banks as well but towards the track and around the Tote sales cabins there was a common freedom and a common intercommunication of which horse was going to win. Sadly, many Chinese, with their obsession for gambling, did not fare well and suicides were not unheard of after a racing season.

My circle of friends spread out from the girls at Secretarial School. Valerie became my girlfriend and her best friend Laura's boyfriend was Tom, the soldier I have mentioned earlier. He and I were both golfers and we used to thoroughly enjoy taking a day off and driving out to Fan Ling in the New Territories or over the Peak to the Shek O golf course at the southeast of the island. With the girls, we would take the yacht out sailing or have an evening out cruising thorough Wan Chai, which, like Yau Ma Tei off Nathan Road in Kowloon, was a lively area full of restaurants, street food vendors, bars and brothels. On other evenings, we would visit the cinema, almost a weekly ritual.

One of the limitations of being a boy teenager going out with a girl teenager is that you both live at home. We had the yacht but we were always on it with friends and the boat boy. Our amorous attentions to each other were limited to kissing and cuddling in the cinema or more adventurously on the yacht. We decided something had to be done.

My first real girlfriend, Valerie, enjoying refreshment

Chapter 60

Over dinner one evening, we decided that the four of us would go to Macau. I have no idea now how we managed to get parental approval, but we did, and the four of us set off on the ferry to Macau.

We hired motorcycles and set off for a tour of the island before settling into our hotel inappropriately named the Hotel Homo. It was now dusk so we took a quick meal accompanied by a couple of bottles of wine and headed back to the hotel where we bid Tom and Laura goodnight. We did not see them again until about midday the next morning.

Macau was originally Portugal's outpost in China and the small town, other than the main street, was rather run down but here and there were remnants of Portuguese architecture and an attractive church. The centre of the town was the main street and its plethora of gambling casinos – the essential Macau.

It was fascinating to watch the Chinese and their obsession with gambling particularly for the game of fan-tan which was played on the table on the ground floor. But, above the ground floor were two to three higher floors with balconies from which straw baskets full of money were lowered to the tables below. It seemed that virtually every gambling game ever invented was available – roulette, blackjack, poker, mah-jong and many others. The couple of casinos we visited were packed not only with Chinese but with a variety of tourists, many of whom were either other eastern nationalities or Australians.

I had never had much desire to gamble and this excess confirmed me in my decision to have, perhaps, a fiver on a horse race or be prepared to lose a few pounds if out with other gambling friends.

Besides, I had a far more beautiful and interesting activity in which to happily indulge with a more than willing companion.

After our weekend, we took the ferry back to Hong Kong to resume our normal life style though the trips in the yacht became just for one couple with the boat boy relegated to the rear of the boat and the cabin door firmly closed.

Valerie with our friends at the entrance to the strangely named but
to me memorable Hotel Homo

Chapter 61

Hong Kong's media was quite limited. The main paper, published in both English and Cantonese, was the South China Morning Post. The main radio service was that of the BBC, again broadcasting in both languages. There were two competitors to the BBC, Rediffusion and Commercial. In 1957, Radio Rediffusion had taken the bold step and introduced cable television. It proved to be successful and so the station began to broaden its number of programmes.

September was fast approaching and I received from Rediffusion Television, an offer to join them as a newsreader and interviewer.

I was astonished, surprised and complimented. But what was I to do? In a couple of weeks, I was to fly back to take up my academic life in Dublin. What really troubled me was what would become of me if I stayed in Hong Kong.

I was living a crazy life, a minor celebrity, hard drinking, hard smoking, though so was everybody, spoilt and now offered a chance to continue it.

In the end, I decided to refuse the offer and go to Dublin. The decision was tempered by the fact that I could always come back.

I never did.

The End